THE INSECT ROOM

Felicity Hughes

To Sergio de Isidro,
for all his support and encouragement.

PART ONE

CHAPTER ONE

The van doors clanged open and Caz bolted out into the field. After spending the past few hours festering in a putrid stew of farts, browning apple cores, dog breath and petrol stench, the rush of fresh air felt good. Fearing recapture, Caz increased her speed and flew off down the hill, with Sid barking at her heels and Rosie following close behind.

Reaching the stream at the bottom of the slope, Caz threw herself down on the rough grass, not caring that it prickled her sunburnt skin. Rosie lay down beside her, arms flung wide to embrace the towering clouds that were sailing sedately through the blue sky.

'Get off, mutt,' said Caz, fingers brushing bristly hair as she fended off the panting animal.

Rosie continued to lie on her back, holding a feathery stalk of grass up close to her eyes and watching entranced as the sunlight splintered into tiny rainbows.

'Mum's shouting something,' said Caz, squinting back up the field.

Her younger sister chose to ignore her and continued to lie back spellbound as she examined the fragments of light. Almost white blonde with clear blue dreamy eyes, eight-year-old Rosie sailed through life on a glittering sea of fantasy, the real world slipping by barely noticed. Caz, on the other hand, five years older and just into her teens, saw life all too clearly. She was constantly on the alert, glancing about for signs of danger, wincing slightly, preparing herself for a fatal blow. Imagined slights half heard in the harmless twitter of other children could cut her to the quick. The summer sun that had tanned Rosie's limbs a golden honey brown had fried Caz's pale skin and indelibly stained her face with a splattering of tangerine freckles. Ever vigilant, she held a hand up to shield her eyes from the sun and observed Chris making his way down the slope towards them.

A stick figure stumbling across the field in too big boots and ripped denim. He looked ridiculous, pausing every few steps to sip on his brew and gaze out across the landscape. Hand on hip, his beanstalk frame swayed, ready to go over with the next puff of wind. He drew close and cupped his hands to his mouth, 'Oi oi laides, a word, if you will before we let you off the leash.'

Rosie looked up and trotted over obediently. Chris squatted down and tried to gather them into a scrum. Caz ducked out of his embrace, but Rosie cuddled close, nuzzling her soft blonde head against Chris' matted curls. He smelled appealingly to her of leather, sweat, tobacco and brew.

'Before you scamps go completely feral on us, your mum wanted to remind her precious darlings that you ought to be back at the van by sundown.'

'What happens at sundown?' Rosie said, sticking her fingers into the blim burns in his ratty old t-shirt.

Chris shifted on his haunches, took a drag of his fag and narrowed his eyes, scanning the horizon like a cowboy.

'The bog beast wot roams these parts goes abroad. He especially likes to chew on the flesh of little girls, leaving only a pitiful pile o' bones for yer poor mum to find in the morning.'

His hands snaked out and clutched at her sides sending Rosie into fits of giggles. Caz stood slightly apart and frowned, watching Rosie collapse on the floor in ecstasies of hysterics.

'You don't need to scare her, I'll make sure we get back,' Caz interjected.

Chris glanced up and raised an eyebrow at her then stuck out his tongue. Caz looked away.

'And take that bloody dog wiv' you, your mum n' I are

gonna have a snooze. It's bin a long drive,' he added.

'But mum didn't drive.' Rosie gripped Chris' hand.

'Ah, but she's conserving her strength for the party tomorrow. Now be orf with you, you 'orrible pair and don't get into no bother with no farmers.'

He stood up and started shambling back up the hill, ragged smoke streaming out behind him.

******

Silvery dandelion spores drifted by on warm air currents. Steeped in the golden glow of early evening sunlight, the countryside cast a spell on them so that they stopped talking. Even the dog stopped barking. When they reached the top of the hill, the ground rolled down again to the dark border of a wood that rose up and swallowed the scenery beyond almost whole, excepting a little hollow in the center where stone turrets held fast in a heaving sea of oak leaves.

Both girls felt the pull of ancient stone walls and, without discussing it, began walking towards the wood. As they got nearer to the trees, they became aware of a faint hum emanating from a barbed wire fence. A mess of feathers and clean bone dangled from a rusted spike. As if it were welcoming them, the dead bird's skull was cracked open with a broken grin.

'It's electric. We better go back,' said Caz.

But Rosie, who had already dragged a big stick over, tuned out her sister's warnings. She levered up the barbed wire at the bottom of the fence.

'We can go through on our tummies.'

'We'll have to tie Sid up.'

They turned to look at the dog. It was wagging its tail excitedly, innocent of the fact that they were both planning to leave it behind.

'You do it Rosie, he likes you.'

'He likes you too.'

Caz knew this was true but avoided touching Chris' mutt if

she could help it. When it wasn't licking her face, it was sticking its head up her skirt and nuzzling her crotch. Rosie, who had the same unquestioning affection for this beast as she did for Chris, didn't argue and instead took the leash from Caz's hand and led him to a small tree that stood a little way apart from the fence.

Rosie crawled under first while Caz levered up the wire, then, taking the stick from her sister, lifted the fence on the other side. Straightening up after crawling along on her belly, Caz came up against a barrier of dense foliage. Thistles and twigs scraped at their skin and Sid's panicked barking tore into the slumbering forest, flustering the birds in the branches above them. After a minute or so they emerged onto a narrow dirt path, dresses stained with green sap and skin covered in scratches. Catching their breath, they listened as the rhythm of Sid's barking slowed to an intermittent aggrieved woofing.

'We should go left,' said Rosie, who had an uncanny knack for knowing the right way. This was the one area in which Caz deferred to her younger sister's judgment. They walked through the woods in single file, Caz taking up the lead, with Rosie hanging close behind, gripping a piece of cloth from the back of her sister's skirt, as if she were afraid that some malevolent force might rip them apart.

The green canopy above rippled with dancing light, and the gentle coo of wood pigeons muffled the noise of Sid's barking, so they weren't even aware when he finally fell silent.

Rosie tugged on Caz's skirt.

'I got stung.' She pointed to a blotchy rash of round white spots that was developing on her ankle. 'Mum says doc leaves are good for stinging nettles,' she added.

They started walking again.

'I don't know what a doc leaf looks like, divvie,' Caz said over her shoulder.

'Grandma says toothpaste is good, we could go back to the van and get some. Or we could take a look in there and see if we can find any.'

The trees cleared to reveal a round red brick house that rose up just above the treetops.

One side of the house was bound in ivy, its windows blinded by sticky emerald-green leaves. If someone didn't chop away the groping tendrils, in a couple of years the rest of the building would be swallowed whole by the plant.

'It's probably crawling with rats,' said Caz.

Rosie, who was teetering on top of a giant rusting lawn roller in order to peer through a ground floor window, chose to ignore her. Crunching gravel and broken glass underfoot, Caz walked around the front of the house and down the path. No one could have driven along there recently without getting their tires ripped up. Overhead, the huge trees loomed, making clacking noises as they heaved in the gentle summer breeze, like ship's sails straining to weigh anchor. The air was heavy and humid and sweat seeped into her armpits.

She turned back to find Rosie and caught the yellow eye of a tabby cat that was sitting near a pile of abandoned junk. Bloody flesh hung from the cat's mouth, the squashed guts of some nameless animal held down with one paw. Frozen for a moment, it stared at Caz, but soon lost interest and went back to chewing stringy red gristle.

'Rosie?'

Her sister had gone. She walked up to the front door. Way above her the top floor windows gleamed gold in the early evening sun, but those lower down were clouded with dust, indifferent to her rising panic. She knew she ought to look through the letter box or cup her hand against a pane of glass, but something held her back. She noticed a large spiderweb spun above the door; it had been some time since anyone had been inside. The door swung inwards and she shouted involuntarily.

Rosie walked out and began to laugh when she saw her sister's surprised face.

'What the fuck,' Caz shouted.

Rosie carried on laughing, supporting herself on the doorframe. Eventually she was laughing so hard that she had to sit down. It was infectious, and before long Caz had forgotten her anger and was laughing too.

'How did you get in?' she finally managed to say.

'One of the windows was broken. I put my hand through and opened the thingie. Chris says they can't do you if you don't force any locks, it's legal,' Rosie parroted. 'That's how he got our place in Kentish Town.'

The urge to tell her sister off was curbed by her own curiosity, so Caz decided to hold off on delivering a lecture about the dangers of going into empty houses alone.

Inside, the house was hairy with dust, but neat. Someone had carefully squared the place away before leaving. A squat green velvet sofa and matching armchair gave the room a comfortable homely look. This lounge took up most of the space on the ground floor with a tiny crescent-shaped kitchen sliced out back. In the kitchen, Caz found an unplugged fridge, emptied and cleaned, and cupboards stocked with plates, bowls and cups. It seemed as if someone had left the place ready for guests. She opened what looked like a larder door to reveal a narrow flight of stairs leading up to the first floor.

She went up front, with Rosie hanging so close behind that she could hear her sister's shallow breathing. The wooden stairs creaked beneath their weight, making them giggle nervously.

On the first floor they came out on an open-plan room that was almost entirely empty, save for a large wardrobe made from dark wood. Abandoned near the stairs, it looked as if the people who'd lived here had tried to shift it but given up and had been too tired to push it back into place. It was a mystery how they'd got the thing up there in the first place. On this floor the house was engulfed in shadow and this piece of furniture loomed glumly in the half dark. The ceiling hung so low that Caz had to duck to avoid headbutting the light fitting. Rosie went to examine the wardrobe, the mirror on the door reflecting an ever so slightly warped image back. She opened the door.

'It's me,' Rosie exclaimed, pulling out a rag doll with yellow woolen plaits and stitched blue eyes. Caz peered inside the empty wardrobe, it smelled of mothballs.

'I'd put that back where you found it.'

Rosie didn't reply but pouted, holding the doll close.

'Let's check the rest of the house first, just to make sure we're alone.'

The final flight of stairs stood at the other end of the room. Caz paused at the bottom and looked back, waiting for Rosie to join her. Reluctantly Rosie ditched the doll and followed her up the stairs. They both felt their skin prickling slightly in the shade and, as Caz took hold of the cold metal handle, she shivered. When she threw the door open they were engulfed in a welcome wave of bright light. The windows were shut and the air in the room was thick with a foreign scent that had curdled in the heat. They both made for the window, holding their breath. Caz worked the stiff latch and pushed against the swollen fitting until it gave and the window swung out.

Gasping for air they took in the view: a sea of treetops rippled out in front of them, lapping at the shores of the stately home that sat on a hill beyond.

'I own a castle,' said Rosie flinging her arms out wide.

'I own a stately home,' shouted Caz, also embracing the prospect with outstretched arms. 'It's not a castle stupid. I get dibs.'

It was a game that Tink had started. Whenever they went somewhere new she would fling her arms out wide and shout, 'I own the mountains. I own the trees. I own the sky!' After mimicking her for a while, the game had devolved into calling dibs. On the way down in the van they'd called dibs on Porsches, Harley Davidsons, Lamborghinis and BMWs. The rule was that they had to throw their arms out wide, shout 'I own...' and call that thing by its proper name. In the last couple of weeks on the road, helped by Chris, they'd acquired an impressive knowledge of car makes and models. If there was no arbitrator, this all led to a huge amount of squabbling. This irritated Tink, who, by trying to challenge the idea of private ownership, had inadvertently given her kids an appetite for material possessions.

'Of course, you can come and live with me in my stately home. I'll let you have a lady's maid from my staff,' said Caz.

'She could do my hair in a French plait every morning.'

'And we could have all our friends over to stay from London. I could invite Ellie and you could ask Patrick.'

'I think I'd invite Samantha instead. Patrick is always breaking things.'

'You're right, we don't want him breaking the china,' Caz concurred.

Caz imagined servants ranged down the stairs in front of the classic portico, standing to attention as they greeted them on their arrival. The sun hung just off to the right of the house, huge and orange in the evening sky.

A loud bang downstairs made Caz yell out in shock. They turned and fled down the stairs, running all the way down to the living room to find that the front door had banged shut behind them. They tried the door to make sure they weren't locked in. There was nobody outside and the cat had disappeared. Just as her heart was beginning to slow, a dark shape skittered across the floor into the kitchen. Caz screamed and dragged Rosie from the house. In the distance Sid began to bark in alarm. As if something had crawled onto her skin and she couldn't shake it off, Caz did a little jig around the garden.

Rosie stood watching her sister.

'I saw something, something big run into the kitchen. I think it was a rat. Can we just get out of here?' Caz said breathlessly.

'It was a cat, Caz,' Rosie said. 'I saw it outside. It must have come in after us.'

'I'm not going back in there.'

Rosie took her sister's hand and they walked together back through the trees, Caz jumping every time they heard a bird rustling in the bushes. She had a thing about rats.

'I forgot the doll,' said Rosie.

'Listen to Sid, he's going off his nut, we've got to go and calm him down.'

'And then go back for the doll?'

'It's getting late. Mum will wonder where we are.'

'I want that doll.' Rosie had come to a halt and stood there, quietly defiant.

'We'll go back tomorrow. We can take Sid and he'll scare the rats away.'

'Promise?'

'Cross my heart, etc.,' Caz said, though she'd rather have stuck a needle in her own eye than go back into that house. Still, they'd be busy with the party tomorrow, so she supposed that with any luck Rosie would forget all about it.

CHAPTER TWO

Chris smacked the package down and the trestle table wobbled under the weight of dead flesh. Whatever it was, was smeared in blood and wrapped in plastic.

'What the hell is that?' demanded Caz.

'It's the head of the bog beast wot I just slayed down in the woods,' Chris replied.

Rosie screamed and hid behind Caz, grabbing at her clothes till Caz shook her off in frustration.

'It isn't a beast,' whispered Rosie at a volume barely audible to the others.

'Just you come and take off this 'ere plastic and see for yourself,' Chris challenged in his mock yokel accent.

He lit up a cigarette and stood back satisfied. Caz thought that he didn't make a very convincing beast killer; if you stuck him on a stick in the middle of a field, he wouldn't even be very good at scaring the crows away.

'Stop teasing the kids.'

Tink floated out towards them on a cloud of purple perfume, the hem of her Indian skirt grazing the ground. She ripped off the plastic and jumped back screaming.

The worst thing about it was that it was smiling at them. Despite not having a body, the 50lb pig's head was grinning, just like the Cheshire cat in Alice in Wonderland. Its eyes were closed, so clearly the joke was a private one. Sid started barking in alarm.

'What the fuck do you propose to do with that then?' shouted Tink.

'Make a stew, it's cheap grub. I learnt 'ow to do it from Raffy, you know the Brazilian guy in the squat, it's what they eat in the barrio in Rio de Janeiro. We just need an 'ammer so we can smash its 'ead in.'

Rosie yelped and clapped her hands over her ears singing. 'La la la la....'

'Have you completely lost it? Half the crowd's veggie,' pointed out Tink. 'Besides I don't want you wasting the gas on cooking up some nasty stew.'

'Well, we could put the head on a stick and have him as a mascot,' suggested Chris, beginning to droop, stick limbs collapsing in.

Tink began to laugh.

'Where did you get that horrible thing anyway?'

'Farmer gave it me as a present,' said Chris. 'Thought it rude to decline,' he added, looking to Tink for approval.

'Well, I hope it's the only pig we see this evening,' said Tink.

'Amen to that.' Chris looked around, paranoid that if they spoke of the devil, he'd be sure to come sniffing around. So far, the only faces turning up had been familiar ones from the party circuit. He clapped his hands to dispel the bad vibes. 'So, can I rely on the world's cutest roadies to help me set things up then?'

When Caz pointed out they were also the world's most underpaid roadies he simply tousled her hair and suggested she join a union. After dumping several plastic carrier bags full of wires at the bottom of the field, she slunk off back to the trailer and, checking no one was about, opened up her book.

She'd borrowed it off her friend from school. Angela's parents were Catholic so the picture on the front of a man's hand cupping a lady's jodhpur-clad bottom had been hidden with a homemade cover of pretty pink floral wallpaper. Not wanting to get teased by the others, Caz had left the cover on. It was the second time she'd read it. She'd just got to the bit where the redheaded heroine Helen goes to her first horse race, when there was a gentle knock at the door.

'Love, can I have a quick word?'

She put the book under the covers of her bed.

'What is it?' she shouted.

Tink opened the door and peeked in.

'Can I come in?'

Her mother's timidity drove her mad.

'It's your trailer, isn't it?'

Like the trailer was some kind of sanctum, Tink pushed the door open and sat down, slowly removing her wellies and placing them outside before entering in stockinged feet. The glass bangles round her wrists and bells on her ankles jingled as she padded across the floor. Lucky thing Caz had insisted they didn't put one of Tink's Indian statues in there, otherwise she'd be start kowtowing to it like a madwoman.

'Rosie not with you?' she asked, sitting beside her eldest daughter on the bed.

'She's helping Chris.'

'It's lovely here, right, like being a princess in the Arabian nights with all these nice fabrics. Aren't you glad you're not spending the summer in the smelly old London?'

Caz communicated the depths of her apathy and disdain with a shrug and a grunt.

Giving up on selling the experience to her daughter, she changed tack and her voice became wheedling.

'So, I don't want to lay anything massive on you or anything, but you're in charge tonight, right? Chris and I are gonna be really busy, so I'm relying on you to keep Rosie in line, okay?'

Wrong, thought Caz. It irritated her off that she always got the blame if anything happened, but she gave her grudging assent anyway with the tiniest of nods.

'You're so sorted, it's great to know I can rely on you.' Tink grappled Caz in an awkward hug. Caz could feel the bird-like frailty of her body beneath the floaty fabrics she wore. She wished she had a mum who was stricter, more substantial, one that enforced boundaries beyond which it was unsafe to stray.

Gazing out of the trailer window at the darkening sky, she caught sight of Chris stomping on an old wooden pallet for firewood.

'Let's go out and give him a hand, eh?' Tink said following Caz's gaze. 'It'll be nice to get round the fire and catch up with everyone.'

******

Rosie had drifted off into a trance, staring at the flames licking the side of the cot. A twisted bundle of cloth inside gave the impression that they were attending some kind of sacrifice. The group sat gathered around the fire either cross legged on the ground, or balanced on plastic beer crates. A busted sofa had even materialized by the fireside, though nobody, except Baz, who didn't seem to care about the mushrooms growing beside him, would occupy it.

Baz came from Glasgow and had a slurred and guttural accent that made them laugh, but also scared them a bit. Already halfway through his third can of Strongbow, his speech was so blurred with booze that Caz had only a vague impression of what he was talking about. It was like looking out of the window on a stormy day, the view warped by raindrops on the windowpane.

'Baz, you going to fry up some of those mushrooms you're growing tomorrow morning,' quipped Chris.

Baz's head wobbled for a second and slowly swung round to contemplate the growths coming out of the sofa's busted seams.

'I goh me own eca-sistem gain on, right?' He laughed to reveal a terrifying set of gnashers. Worn down with decay, they were almost pointed, like fangs.

Tink said that Baz was a sweetheart, but the girls still shrank from him. Even when he offered them polo mints, holding them out in his dirty cracked hand, big brown eyes glistening like a dog waiting to be patted on the head, they usually backed away, saying, *thanks but mum doesn't let us eat sweets*, leaving Baz looking sad and mystified. Tink had told them that his kids were in care, their mother had been a junkie and the social had taken them away when they'd tracked Baz down on site.

'Where d'you find it?' asked Tink, pointing to the cot.

There were a bunch o' this kiddie stuff jist left by the road. Looked like it'd bin there fer ages n' all.'

'I could have done with some of that stuff,' said Tink. 'Wish you'd told me before you burnt it.'

'Ach, it'd bin there fer ages, some puir fuck pro'bly wanted rid o' it. 'Sides, this stuff has bad vibes, best burned.' Baz's eyes brimmed with tears.

'It's top-quality gear though, must have set them back a bob or two,' Chris pointed out.

Baz waved his hand dismissively, he wanted rid of the subject. He took a long pull on his bottle.

'Bet it belonged to the people in the castle,' piped up Rosie.

'Castle?' Tink turned and looked at her daughter.

'There's a castle over there, we saw it today,' she began, then trailed off after catching a warning look from Caz.

******

The speakers crackled on, briefly filling the field with dead noise before the bass kicked in. It rattled the thin walls of their trailer, making the girls snuggle deeper inside their sleeping bags. It was only 8:30, but Caz and Rosie were already laid out on the narrow mattresses that lined each side of the trailer, staring up at the printed Indian fabrics that floated above their heads.

At first, they'd stayed up for the parties. But they didn't like the way complete strangers grinned at them, their teeth glowing fluorescent against the dark. Rosie had been close to tears once when someone they didn't know had picked her up and swung her round. Then there'd been the guy with the bright red skin and only one tooth who had stuck his face close up to theirs and started howling incomprehensibly.

The other kids ran around wild in a big gang so the adults couldn't interfere with them, but Caz steered clear of them, ever since Peanut, the skinhead kid with the glass eye, had asked her out on a date a few weeks ago. They'd all stood behind him to watch when he had, and the joke had seemed to be on her.

Illuminated by the fairy lights that hung from the ceiling, the grubby interior of the van was almost cosy. Familiar domestic objects that appeared cheap and battered in the cold light of day took on a comforting glow, reassuring Caz that they were safe inside the flimsy metal walls of the trailer.

Rosie sat up in bed and reached under her pillow for her red plastic handbag. It was an evening ritual with her to go through its contents: the strawberry sticker that smelled of real strawberries, a tiny metal dolphin, a dried flower preserved in a piece of clear plastic, a large jet-black marble, a tiny purse that contained a lock of her best friend's hair and a Moroccan coin. The order of service was to lay each of these treasures out on the duvet before bedtime, muttering secret incantations to her Cindy doll all the while. When she came to the black marble, she'd place it in her palm and stare into it intently. That evening was no different.

'What do you see in your crystal ball tonight Madame Rosamund?' asked Caz.

Rosie ignored her as usual and, after a minute of intent observation, began packing her amulets away again. Caz often found herself feeling unnerved when her sister got like this.

'We never went back for the doll,' whispered Rosie.

'We can always go tomorrow morning, before the adults get up. Best time really.'

Rosie didn't answer but instead whispered something to Cindy.

CHAPTER THREE

C az woke up to the sound of angry shouts. It had just begun to get light outside and the sky was sickly and wan, streaked with dirty grey cloud. The music had stopped. She sat up and looked over at Rosie's empty bed. Pulling on her mum's parka over her pajamas, she slipped on a pair of wellies and headed outside.

A woman was squatting down for a piss beside the trailer.

'Alright,' called the peeing lady, falling backwards into the mud as she struggled to pull up her pants. 'Oops,' she said, cackling with glee at the situation. Caz locked the van, pocketed the key to the padlock and turned her back on this post party casualty, striding off down the hill. Dazed revelers stumbled up the slope towards her, but she avoided eye contact with these grey faced gurning ghouls.

As she scanned the crowd at the bottom of the hill for her mum, she caught sight of the police vans. Chris' decks and sound system had gone, and a slagging match was going on between the white-faced impassive police and an outraged knot of travelers. On the fringes, Caz found her tear-stained mum clinging to her friend Mags' arm.

'Mum,' Caz called.

Tink glanced about her till she caught sight of her daughter.

'Caz love. They've gone and taken Chris' van,' she wailed.

'Fucking pigs,' Mags shouted loud enough for the police to hear.

'Where's Chris then?' asked Caz.

'He's been arrested and his van's been confiscated along with all his gear,' said Tink.

Caz sighed and took her mum's hand. 'Shall I make a cup of tea?'

'Thanks love,' her mum sniveled, wiping her eyes with her tattered sleeve.

******

They walked up the hill together in silence after saying goodbye to Mags.

Caz opened up the trailer and got the fold up chairs out from inside, so that Tink could have a sit down. Popping back inside, she brought out the camping gas, filled a kettle with bottled water and got it going.

'Chamomile?'

Her mum nodded and Caz ducked back inside the van for mugs and teabags, finally remembering when she looked at Rosie's empty bed that her sister was still missing. She'd forgotten to look for her.

'Mum, did Rosie go with Chris?'

'What love? Rosie, no. Wasn't she with you?'

'Hold on, she must still be down at the party.'

Before her mum had time to answer, Caz tore off down the hill, heart pounding in her chest. There was hardly anyone left now. The local revelers had mostly gone or were passed out in misshapen lumps on the edges of the field and the travelers had either returned to their vans or been taken to town by the police.

She looked around desperately, scared to ask strangers about her sister, but equally terrified to go back empty handed. The pig's head was jammed down onto a stick, slightly askew. It grinned at the devastated scene, eyes alive with swarming flies.

CHAPTER FOUR

T he sign on the gate read, Trespassers will be prosecuted. Tink didn't pause before lifting the rusty metal catch and pushing aside the bolt. They hadn't gone under the fence because Tink had pointed out that Rosie wouldn't have been able to lift it alone, instead they'd walked along, looking for another point of entry, eventually coming upon this dirt track.

The trees above whispered in the breeze and Caz could almost make out the word, *trespassers*.

'I put you in charge,' Tink said, breaking her silence to remind Caz that the blame lay squarely on her shoulders. They continued up the path, wellies sinking into thick brown mud, at one point suckering Caz's boot so fast that her foot came right out. Tink did not wait for her to extract the boot, but trudged ahead, forcing Caz to run awkwardly through the mire to catch her back up. They must have missed a turn because the road eventually opened out on a gravel drive that swept up to the grand house Caz had seen over the treetops.

'We'll have to ask directions,' Tink said.

'But we're not allowed here.'

'Bollocks,' replied Tink.

In the middle of the lawn was an enormous fountain and behind it the mansion. Glazed in honey-coloured sunlight, the stone house looked appetising, like you could break off a piece to eat. Caz's stomach gurgled and she remembered that she hadn't had any breakfast. She counted 20 windows just on the front and wondered how many people were inside, whether they were still asleep. She remembered a visit to a stately home with her grandmother one tranquil summer's day. She'd seen her first peacock and eaten strawberry ice cream in a café. But that place had been full of snap happy day trippers in colourful clothes; the grounds of this house were deserted except for the huge stone figures throwing frozen poses in the fountain. Maybe it was too early for visitors.

Caz counted 15 steps up to the door. Despite her size, Tink took them two at a time. At the top Tink pressed the ivory doorbell and it gave out a weak little chirrup, like a chick fallen from the nest.

'I think you've got to push harder,' Caz suggested.

She tried again, putting all of her weight behind it, and this time it gave off a hard metallic trill that lasted for several seconds. They waited, Caz realizing that she should have changed out of her pyjamas before setting off. She zipped up her parka over the pastel pink cotton fabric. Tink was about to ring again, but as she raised her finger, the door swung open.

'Can I help you?' the voice was sonorous and smooth with well-rounded vowels.

'Sorry to bother you, but I've lost my kid,' said Tink. 'A little girl, eight years old. We come from the camp over there.'

'Ah.' The man looked off over their heads towards the trees. It was difficult for Caz to see his face from up close, instead she found herself looking up into a pair of nostrils dilating and contracting.

'Only, we think she might have gone into your woods. It seems that she was looking for a house, not this house, a round house, out in the woods.'

'You better come in,' he opened the door, but kept his arm barred across, so that they had to duck under to enter. As soon as they were inside, he slammed it shut behind them, plunging them into darkness.

'This way please.'

A chill rose from the stone slabs that paved the hall, giving

Caz goosebumps.

They blindly followed the shadowy figure across the dark hall, his footsteps tapping lightly in front of them, before entering a sunny room that overlooked the grounds.

'Sit,' he said, adding, 'please,' as an afterthought.

They sat down in a pair of padded leather seats. The leather squeaked when they moved, so instead of getting comfortably settled, both sat stiffly to attention, as if they were in a headmaster's office.

The tall man sat opposite them. The morning sunlight was streaming through the window, but sitting back in the shadows, the man's face was obscured. Now all Caz could see of him were his hands: smooth white long fingers and square well-polished nails. Sitting folded one on top of the other in his lap, they were motionless except for a thumb that constantly moved with the jerky motion of a broken clockwork toy.

'I found a little girl who I presume must be your daughter wandering around my grounds in the early hours. I took her in for her own good. She's perfectly safe. In fact, she's playing out in the back of the house. I...' The voice stuck for a second and the thumb halted mid-air. 'I was about to report it to the police when you turned up.'

'Good thing we arrived when we did then,' Tink said, beginning to stand. 'Where is she?'

'You'll see her presently. I'd just like to have a little chat first,' said the man.

'I don't see there's anything to talk about.'

'Aren't you.' Another pause, the man breathed laboriously as if it were an effort to get the words out and the thumb jutted skywards, stuck again. 'Ah ah, aren't you just the slightest bit worried that she spent part of the night in a stranger's house, for instance?'

'Course, that's why I want to see her.'

'Don't you ah, don't you even want to ask me some questions? Or is this a regular event?'

'Listen mate, you're seriously out of line, I take good care of my kids.'

'I'm sorry, I know this must be painful for you. I'm just concerned that your daughter went missing in the middle of the night and this morning is the first I hear from you.'

Tink had sat back down with the air of a naughty schoolgirl and was now wrapping her fingers round and round the tassels on her skirt, binding them tightly, then letting the thread unravel, leaving behind sharp white lines in her skin.

'Caz was in charge of looking after her,' said Tink.

The man turned his attention to Caz, who pulled her parka down over her pink pyjama bottoms. She was hot and flushed.

'Ah.' He cleared his throat; the thumb rose and fell regularly, settling into a rhythm. 'Caz. You are Rosie's older sister I presume?' He didn't wait for an answer. 'Are you often left in charge of her all night?'

Caz glared at him. When their dad had left there'd been a few people asking questions about Tink's parenting skills. She wasn't about to give them the satisfaction then and she definitely wouldn't let anything slip now.

'No, but...'

'Last night was different, we had a crisis. Can I please see my daughter now?' Tink butted in.

'What kind of a crisis? It sounded more like you were all having a nice little party on my land.' The thumb accelerated.

'Did you call the cops on us?' shouted Tink, her voice hysterically rising and breaking with panic.

'Were the police called?' The man unfolded his hands briefly to pick some fluff off his trousers and folded them back one on top of the other once they'd swept away the lint. The thumb slowed, now caressing instead of tapping his wrist.

'Perhaps they had some concerns about the legality of your party? Hmmm.'

Tink glared out of the window, all the time the thread on her finger tightened till the skin underneath went white and tears began to well up in her eyes.

The man leaned forward, his face penetrating the field of

sunlight. Smooth and pale, the skin on his forehead was almost transparent so that a vein that flashed a blue lightning bolt down the centre was all the more disturbing. His eyes were the same arresting colour blue, and when they briefly swept over in Caz's direction, they seemed to zap her motionless, sending shivers down her spine. She looked at the wooden floor: saw fluid amber lines rippling out in whirlpool patterns that seemed to draw the eye into ever decreasing circles.

'I suppose you've had a very hard night. You can, however, understand my concerns.' Now he had gained the upper hand, his voice flowed out and enveloped them, as richly textured as the wood.

Tink nodded her head, chastised, her face reddening, tears now streaming down her cheeks. Then to Caz's horror, she started wailing, just like Rosie had done when she fell in the river and hit her head.

Caz felt scared. *She's really losing it this time*, she thought.

The man leaned forward and took Tink's hand. His tongue darted out to wet his thin lips, as if he were ready to devour her.

'You can understand my concerns, hmmm. There's no telling what trouble children can get into these days, no?'

The vein began to pulse so that when he leaned back into the shadows and the slice of sunlight again divided them, Caz sighed with relief.

'So, tell me Caz, how old are you?'

His voice was somehow enhanced in the darkness.

'Thirteen,' she muttered. She kept her eyes locked on the thumb as it beat out time; he now seemed to be controlling the pace of the conversation with it.

'And where do you live?'

'London,' she replied.

'Where do you go to school?'

'Kentish Town. We're off for the summer though.' Caz glanced at Tink for reassurance.

'I know what you're thinking, we're not gypsies, we're just out and about in the van this summer,' Tink put in.

Suddenly the hands sprang into action and Caz yelped. The man had slapped his thigh.

'How marvellous, you're one of those new age travellers. I've read all about you in the papers. I must apologize, this is one of the first times I've met any of your ilk. I suppose, you must find me terribly rigid, hmm,' he said, leaning in close again.

'No no,' protested Tink, shrinking back in her chair.

'No, but put yourself in my place, a small child turns up in the middle of the night, distressed, her parents nowhere to be found. Under normal circumstances you would have turned up sooner, but I suppose you were in a spot of hot water. Hmm?'

He leaned forward and placed a hand on Tink's to prevent her cutting off her blood supply with a fatal twirl of the finger.

Tink nodded, a slurry of snot gurgling in her nose as she sniffed in the affirmative. 'It's the police. They've impounded Chris' van. I mean Chris, my partner's van.'

'Rosie's father?

'No, he's just my partner. He organized the whole thing really,' Tink said with a hint of pride.

'So, what are you going to do?'

'He'll be out in a bit, I guess. He didn't break any laws.'

'Do you have anywhere to sleep?' he asked, voice oily with affected sympathy.

'We've got the trailer. We can squeeze up and sleep there.'

'I mean, anywhere to park it.'

'Well, I thought we'd just stay in the field...'

'Hmmm. Listen, I'd like to help you out. Why don't you come and park on the grounds instead?'

'We couldn't, but if you let us, we'll stay on the field.'

'I can't have you living out there with two young girls, no running water and electricity, especially when the solution is easy. There's the old caretaker's house just a way back off the driveway, the round house you were looking for in fact. It's not occupied, you could use the facilities. You could even sleep there. It would be much better for the children don't you think? I couldn't bear to think of them out there in such conditions.'

Tink started looking about her as if for a means of escape.

'You don't have to decide now, let's go and find Rosie, shall we? I bet you're worried sick. The name's Lacy by the way, Rupert Lacy.'

He stood up and offered Tink his hand. Tink accepted and got to her feet, pink eyes timidly cast to the ground.

'I'm Emma, but everyone calls me Tink. It's short for Tinkerbell, because I'm always tinkling see.' She jangled the bangles on her arm and laughed weakly.

Lacy stared down, cobalt eyes glowing with a look of triumph as she trailed off. He waited a second before drawling, 'How charming, but whatever is wrong with Emma? It's a lovely name.'

He glanced over and caught Caz's eye. Instead of smiling or turning away, looked at her steadily, as if he were gazing out of a window but thinking of something else entirely. Fixed with that far-away stare, she felt as if she was gradually fading, becoming as transparent as glass. Without a flicker of emotion crossing his face, he turned from her and led them out into the house.

The mansion, too, with its ancient dark stone floors and oak walls, cut her down to size. Caz felt the need to make a stronger impression by banging her feet on the floor as they walked down the corridor, but she was forced to stop when she almost slipped on a loose slab.

'Careful.' Lacy's voice echoed in the cavernous space. 'We're falling into rack a ruin a bit here.'

After crossing a gloomy room filled with oversized pieces of furniture that slumbered under white sheets, Lacy opened a door into a small lounge where they found Rosie folded in upon herself, nestled in a window ledge, intent on brushing the hair of a doll. She looked up briefly when they entered.

'Rosie, your mum has come to find you.' Lacy placed a hand on her shoulder.

'But I thought we were going to see if you had more clothes for the dolly,' she lisped, turning and looking at him.

'Rosie, I've been out of my mind.' Tink rushed forward and

wrapped her arms around her daughter.

'Hello,' replied Rosie, not at all pleased to see her mum.

'Where've you been?' demanded Caz.

Rosie looked up at her sister dreamily.

'Oh, Caz,' she said, as if she'd just remembered that she had a sister.

'Where're your clothes?' Caz asked.

She was dressed in a plain blue cotton t-shirt and floral print skirt. Simple, but expensive looking.

'It's Laura Ashley,' Rosie said, holding the fabric out between her fingers.

'Rosie's clothes were filthy when she arrived here so Mrs Dixon, my housekeeper, gave her some of my daughter's old things to wear this morning,' said Lacy.

'We ought to go find Chris.' Tink tried to keep hold of Rosie, who was squirming away, wriggling out of her grip, before clamping herself to Lacy's side. Lacy sunk his fingers into her blonde curly hair and Caz thought of a documentary she'd seen on octopuses wrapping their tentacles around their prey.

'Of course,' said Lacy. 'How about we drive your trailer over first?'

He was really into the idea of moving them.

'But we need to find Chris,' whispered Tink.

'Well, how about Bill, my caretaker, gives you a lift to Barchester police station after he's moved you? Let me call the police right away and see if we can't find out where he is,' Lacy said, playing the sensible parent to Tink's whimsical child.

'We don't want to be any bother,' said Tink. 'But it might be safer for the kids...'

'Great, tell you what, Bill will help you fetch the van after we call the police.'

******

Bill, like the Land Rover he drove, looked like he spent all day sploshing about in mud. But it didn't seem like this activity gave him any joy. His mouth flatlined, making it impossible to detect any sign of life in his lips when he spoke, and the terse phrases he mumbled may as well have been in ancient Egyptian for all Caz understood.

'Arwp in.'

The three of them – Tink, Rosie and Caz – stared at Bill confused until he jerked his head towards the van.

Before they'd even got their seatbelts done up, he'd let out the clutch so that the van, as if it'd been a huge dog straining at the leash, lurched forward. Once they'd turned off the drive onto country track, it began to bump up and down as it hit potholes in the road. But Bill, seeming to derive a grim joy at their discomfort, increased the speed and before they knew it, they'd come out onto the main road and were bowling into the field.

Besides their trailer, only a couple of vehicles remained of the camp and those that had been left behind were packing up and preparing to leave. Tink got out of the car and went to talk to Mags.

'I don't want to stay in that house,' Caz said, slightly surprised at herself for speaking these words out loud.

'No, won't catch me staying in thair neither,' Bill mumbled.

The slack flesh across his cheeks tightened for a second, betraying some suppressed emotion.

Caz glanced back to see if his words had registered with her sister. But Rosie was spacing out as usual, staring up at the clouds in the sky, her consciousness floating high up above, only tenuously attached to her body.

CHAPTER FIVE

Outside Barchester's police station there was a festive atmosphere. The travellers had erected a small protest camp on the pavement opposite decorated with Honk Your Horn for Justice and Free to Party banners. Sat out on lawn chairs, they soaked up the sun and the undivided attention of the town's inhabitants. A gang of fresh-faced teenage kids wearing Doc Martins and distressed jeans were hanging out nearby, desperately trying to blend in and shake off their middle-class taint. Even the local goths had shuffled over from smoking behind gravestones to take a look.

Although the police had released the travellers from custody after a few hours, their sound equipment and vans remained confiscated.

'Fucking travesty,' declared Red, a local political agitator who had offered to put them up in his lounge and hadn't had this much fun since the road protest last year. Chris was also enjoying himself. An old lady had brought them out cakes and tea, a gesture which had touched him far more than Red's show of solidarity.

'French fuckin' fancies, absolutely blinding,' he said, recounting the tale with relish to Tink and the kids when they turned up.

A busload of posh schoolgirls rushed past, the occupants screaming their support out the windows as if they were at a rock concert. Chris waved back, nonchalantly riding the wave of teenage adulation. He cracked open a can and reached over to cuddle Rosie, who squirmed out of his embrace.

'She thinks I've forgotten her,' he said.

'Rosie's had a scare, or rather, she gave us a bit of a scare. Ran off this morning when the pigs turned up, I got back to find she'd gone. We've been frantic this morning,' said Tink.

'Turned up though didn't she,' Chris said, not wanting to put a dent in his good mood.

'I was frantic I was,' insisted Tink.

'Where was she then?'

'Only at that posh place down the road. He didn't want to let her go when he saw us, did he? Came over high and mighty didn't he Caz?'

Caz didn't feel the need to explain things to Chris or support her mum's version of events, so she kept quiet.

'Hope you gave him what for,' said Chris.

'He's alright. He's letting us stay at his cottage till we get the van back.'

'You said no then,' Chris said.

'Really, he's alright, we've got electricity and running water.'

Chris sat back in his chair and folded his arms, unconvinced.

'It's well wicked, we could have everyone over when you get your van back. We'll be heading off anyway to Tipton, so he won't be able to kick up much of a fuss.'

'I like your thinking you crafty wench. 'Ere, everyone, Tink's got us a place for a house party this week,' he announced to cheers.

PART TWO

CHAPTER SIX

Caz woke up to the liquid noise of pigeons gurgling outside the window. She stared up at the blank ceiling wondering for a brief moment where she was, experiencing a disorientating mental jolt as things clicked into place and she remembered they were in the round house. Rosie was still catatonic, bundled up under sheets at the other end of the mattress. Caz slipped quietly out of bed and padded towards the window.

A light wind blew ripples out over the sea of foliage below and in the distance the manor floated above, catching the first rays of the sun and glowing so richly that it seemed to drift closer and swell in size. It was just gone dawn and the sky was smudged salmon pink. *Shepherd's warning*, thought Caz watching as a flock of birds flew in arrow formation away from the great house.

There was a small bathroom just across the landing. Constellations of grit speckled the bottom of the pea green tub. There hadn't been time to clean it the day before and Caz made a mental note to see if she could find any cream cleaner so she could sort it out later on. After a quick flannel wash in the sink under her pits and between her legs, she looked resentfully at her reflection in the mirror, at the indiscriminate spatter gun spray of freckles. She splashed cold water on them and rubbed with a flannel, as if it were possible to erase them if she scrubbed hard enough. Finally, she ran her wet fingers through her unruly orange curls, smoothing them down for a second, before they bounced right back up again. She yanked hard on a strand, annoyed, then checked herself, letting go and watching as it curled up as tight as a telephone cord.

On the way down to the kitchen she had to pass through the half-dark first floor room. She rushed past the abandoned wardrobe before scurrying down the final flight of stairs and slamming the door behind her.

The ivy hadn't yet smothered the kitchen windows, but still barely any light filtered down through the leafy canopy of the woods outside. Luckily Bill had switched on the electric the day before so she could turn on the light.

She popped an egg into a saucepan, filled it with water and set it down on the stove. While she waited for it to boil, she switched on the old radio. Its sticky surface was caked in a thick layer of dust, so that the large dials were hard to move, but it worked and she managed to get ok reception for Radio One. The cheerful, mildly irritating voice of the DJ restored a sense of normality to the scene. By the time she'd worked out where to angle the antenna for the best reception, the kettle had boiled, and her egg was tapping gently against the bottom of the pan.

She turned down the heat on the egg and set the timer on her digital watch for three minutes, then popped two slices of bread in the toaster. She had a minute or so to make the tea. Careful to heat the pot by swilling, then draining out a dash of hot water, she inserted two teabags before filling it up. She preferred loose tea because Grandma had told her that teabags were made from the scrapings off the factory floor, but Tink wasn't swayed by this argument and said that they didn't need to *put on airs*.

The toast popped up, lightly done, but she didn't want to risk burning it by putting it in again. She glanced at her watch, 43 seconds before the egg was ready. Just enough time to quickly butter her slices, place them on the plate and cut them into soldiers. She hadn't enough time to go rummaging for an eggcup, so she ripped herself one out of the egg carton and spooned the egg out into this improvised container.

'Alphabet Street,' came on the radio. The timing was too

good to be true. Just as she was dipping her first soldier into her perfect runny egg yolk, Rosie entered the kitchen.

Instead of sitting down, she stood nearby.

'Don't hover,' Caz said through a mouthful of buttery crumbs.

'Don't eat with your mouth full,' Rosie primly retorted.

Caz tried to ignore her, instead focusing her attention on her egg. But now she was irritated, she was eating too fast and not enjoying it. A runny egg had to be eaten quickly otherwise it'd go hard, but still, she had no chance to savour it properly with her sister breathing down her neck.

'I can't find the dolly. It's gone. You said we'd go back for it and now it's gone,' Rosie finally said.

'Well, tough. It wasn't your doll in the first place. Why don't you just sit down and eat your breakfast?' Caz said, gesturing towards a box of Sugar Puffs on the kitchen top.

'Could I have French toast?'

Caz finished off her yolk and took a slurp of tea.

'We've only got English toast your highness.'

'No, silly, I mean bread all soggy with egg and fried,' Rosie said, pulling a drawer in and out as she spoke.

'Eggy bread? Why didn't you say so?'

'It's French toast.' Rosie banged the drawer shut hard.

'When did you get all posh?'

Rosie didn't say anything, but sat herself down and looked intently at her sister as if she were attempting to hypnotize her into doing her bidding.

'If you go out to the trailer and give mum a cup of tea, I'll make you some eggy bread. Deal?'

Tink had sunk into one of her moods yesterday. After they'd tidied up the house a bit and got settled in, she'd sloped off to the trailer and sat listening to her Mazzy Star tape over and over again, enveloped in a fug of incense, thoughts circling as she stared into swirling smoke and twirled her hair in her fingers. Caz wasn't too worried; she'd at least got it together to make fish finger sandwiches for dinner before drifting off again.

'She's still asleep,' said Rosie, returning with the tea.

They'd just have to wait it out. After breakfast she crept into the trailer and dug out the scrap paper and box of felt tips for Rosie. Her mother moaned and shifted under the covers but didn't wake.

Back in the sitting room, she handed Rosie the drawing things and flopped down on the sofa with her book. The trees outside rustled and the shadows of leaves rippled in a square of sunlight on the creamy white wall.

It must have been about 11 when she heard a knock at the door. Caz got up to answer it. A teenage boy, a bit taller than she was, stood in front of her. He held his slender body awkwardly, head and hips at an angle and thumbs plugged into the pockets of his jeans. His straight dark hair fell over his eyes and when he tossed his head to get it out of the way, it immediately cascaded back down.

'Um, hi. Is your mum in?' he asked in a posh voice, again tossing his long fringe out of the way.

'She's in the trailer,' said Caz. 'Meditating, we better not disturb her.'

'Um, well, like, my mum wondered if you'd like to come and have some tea, I suppose...' he trailed off.

'Yeah, no right,' said Caz, wondering who his mum was. 'Sorry, who are you?'

'Oh.' He pulled his hair out of his eyes again with his hand. 'I'm Ronnie.'

'Riiiight,' said Caz.

'I'm the housekeeper's son,' he mumbled, hair again obscuring his eyes.

'Insane,' said Caz mimicking a phrase she'd heard from Mags.

Ronnie shuffled, embarrassed at the evident absurdity of his existence.

'This is Rosie.' She gestured to her sister who continued to sit on the floor absorbed in her drawing.

'So, you're staying here?'

'For now,' replied Caz.

'Er, insane.'

Ronnie peeked at her from under his hair and they both laughed.

'Do you like want to have some sandwiches then? They're like fish paste or something.'

'Okay.' Caz looked down to check she hadn't spilt egg yolk on the front of her t-shirt.

******

She left a note on the kitchen table before they headed off. Along the woodland path a cabbage white butterfly lolloped through the air. It seemed to be leading them through the trees but hung back when they reached the wide expanse of green turf that led up to the mansion. It was another sunny day of slowly scrolling white clouds, full of possibility and barely stained with messy family quarrels. Most of the windows winked in the morning sunlight, but Caz noticed that the curtains were drawn on the left-hand side of the building.

'Why are all the curtains shut up there?' she asked.

'Those used to be the nursery and the guest rooms. Upton Park is huge, but it's been mostly empty since Rupert, I mean, Lord Lacy, left for Japan. Even before then that side was totally off limits; the electric went dodgy and the roof began to leak. We live in the other wing, the north wing, at the back of the house. That's mum and me. Lord Lacy is up front.'

Ronnie took them round the right side of the house and down some neat little steps. Worn smooth by centuries of scuffing feet, they sagged slightly in the middle. At the bottom, a pot of bright red geraniums sat beside a small olive-green door.

'Tradesmen's entrance,' said Ronnie, turning and making a face before opening the door.

Inside, a large woman confronted them, her eyes gleaming as she watched them enter. She had a beefy red face and wispy blonde hair that was pasted in places to her broad sweaty forehead. She seemed to fill the room.

'You must be Emma. Lord Lacy has told me all about you.'

'For God's sake mum, this is the other daughter,' said Ronnie.

'Oh, I beg your pardon. I've been chopping onions and can't see a thing.' She laughed. There was an awkward pause.

'Oh, for heaven's sake, then who the hell is she then Ron?' Ronnie's mum said, putting her red fists on pillowed hips.

'Sorry, I didn't get your name,' Ronnie said.

'It's Caz,' she announced to gales of laughter.

'Oh my goodness, WHAT a palaver. Caz my dear, I'm Flora Dixon, I apologize for my idiot son.' She grabbed Ronnie in a headlock.

Ronnie squirmed in his mother's violent embrace. After releasing him she got down on the ground with a lot of huffing and puffing and came level with Rosie.

'Hello my lovely. You've come to visit us again I see and do you know what, you're just in time, I've got a fresh set of sandwiches made up with your name on them.'

Rosie twisted from side to side on one foot and smiled at Mrs Dixon, then let herself be led to the big kitchen table.

'Your mum not about then?' asked Flora, wiping her hands on a dishcloth after she'd placed a dish of sandwiches in front of Rosie.

'She's meditating.'

'Meditating is she? I don't have the foggiest what that's all about, but I suppose it must be nice for her. Only I wanted to ask her if she was set for food. We've got more than enough here. You must let me give you some stuff to tide you over when you leave.'

'That's okay, we went shopping yesterday,' replied Caz.

'Course if your mum's got her own ideas about food that's fine… You're probably all vegetarians no doubt. But we've got some stuff that'll never be used in a month of Sundays so…' Flora trailed off. 'Aren't you all a bit cramped in that trailer you're in?'

Caz felt her face redden.

'Oh, don't mind me. I can be a silly woman sometimes. You just sit down and get some sandwiches down you,' said Mrs Dixon, flushing herself at the sight of Caz's embarrassment.

Caz sat down and reached for a sandwich. It was the posh sort: dainty triangles with the crusts cut off, different fillings of egg mayo, ham and fish paste.

'She's a pretty little thing your sister. Gave us quite a scare though, turning up out of the blue. Lucky we found her when we did. It's not safe to have her wandering off on her own at night.'

Mrs Dixon's voice wobbled slightly and she raised her hand to her mouth, turning away to the window, eyes glazed over with emotion. She sighed, regaining her ballast, huge bosom heaving like the prow of a ship riding a wave.

'So, what's involved with this meditation business?' asked Mrs Dixon, just as Caz took another bite of sandwich.

She tried to answer, but with a face full of sandwich, the crumbs flew out across the table.

'Oh I'm sorry my love, don't answer, I'm a bit of a busybody truth be told. We don't often get colourful folks like yourselves round these parts. I'm just nosy. Ron, weren't you going to show the girls round the house today?'

'Sure, if you're interested.' He shrugged.

Rosie, however, refused to budge and instead clamped herself to Flora's side.

'God sorry, she's such a weirdo.' Caz pulled at her sister's arm.

'Don't you worry. I'd like the company. Why don't you two have a wander and me and Rosie'll make some cakes. About the same age as Ronnie aren't you? He don't have any friends around here no more, it's been ages since he went to school in the village. It'll be nice for him.'

******

'You talk dead posh, not a bit like your mum.'

Caz's voice rang out across the gloomy hallway. She

sounded hard, bitchy and ignorant. Always on the defensive, she was already spoiling things before they'd even had a chance to begin.

'Well, I don't really live here. I go to school at Ardingly. If I spoke like the bumpkins round here, I'd be pulverized in an instant.'

'Why don't you go to a normal school?'

'Lord Lacy thinks a good education is important, he helps with my fees.'

Caz's plastic sandals squeaked on the polished floor, an institutional noise she remembered from gym class. It made her feel small. She felt in her pocket for her lip balm, popped off the cap and spread it on her lips, inhaling the comforting strawberry scent.

Ronnie leaned back on an expensive dark wood table.

'Would you like to see the insect room?'

'Sure.'

He walked up the stairs running a hand over the wide banister. She wondered if he'd ever slid down it. If he had, he probably didn't anymore, he was too grown up. They arrived at a landing and turned right through an archway that opened out onto a long gallery.

Caz peered at the pictures that lined the walls. Though the people in the frames all wore clothes from a different era, the resemblance was still clear in the way they held themselves: drawing themselves up to their full height, chests puffed out, noses tilted upwards and eyes looking sideways and down at you with a hint of pity.

'Do the eyes start moving when no one's around?' said Caz.

'Do you know they might, but I've never caught them at it,' Ronnie laughed.

'Who's little Bo Peep then?' she said pointing to a portrait of a pink-cheeked lady in a frilly frock.

'That's Lady Marguerite Lacy. She was French, married into the family and died of pneumonia shortly afterwards.'

'Is there a picture of Lord Lacy, I mean the guy who is Lord

Lacy now?'

'Only as a child. They never had a family portrait done.'

They reached the end of the corridor and Ronnie led her down a few steps through another doorway. Inside was a long low room lined with flat glass cabinets. Behind the glass, rows of butterflies and beetles were pinned to yellowing paper. It was the life's work of a meticulous person; a person with sloping handwriting who probably wore a monocle as he carefully wrote up each label. Ronnie trailed his long fingers along the wooden frames of the glass cases, and let his eyes pass over the rows of tiny corpses.

'Some of these are from as far away as Peru. The current Lord Lacy's great uncle Francis was a passionate entomologist. He hunted them in the jungle. Carefully laid each one out,' Ronnie explained.

'How did he kill them?'

'A rag of chloroform in a killing jar, they simply go to sleep. There's still some in the cupboard, see.' He pointed to a dingy looking brown bottle in a cabinet. 'Rupert keeps the key though.'

A faint sweetish odour tickled the back of Caz's throat. She tried to open a window, but found they were painted shut.

'It's powerful stuff, you can knock an adult out with it, but what they don't tell you on the TV shows is that it can also give you burns if you don't use it right, even kill someone in a high enough dose.'

'Does Mister Lacy collect anything?'

Ronnie looked up at her.

'Swords, *katana* from Japan, they're terribly valuable, fatal too, in the wrong hands. Samurai warriors would lop off their enemies' heads with a single stroke. I'll show you if you like, but it has to be our secret, I'm not even allowed to go in there. You have to treat them with respect. Some people think they're cursed by the ghost of dead samurai.'

'Yeah yeah.'

'Want to see?'

She couldn't back out, so she nodded, despite the fact that

her heart was thumping out a warning.

To get to Lord Lacy's private rooms they had to go up two floors and further out to side of the house. Creeping silently along the corridors, Ronnie led the way. When Caz tried to ask a question, he turned round and put his fingers to his lips.

The smell in the house kind of reminded her of the squat in Kentish Town; a funny dry scent of things shut in for too long. The carpets hadn't been vacuumed in ages, and the air was filled with drifting clouds of slowly falling dust. The cream wallpaper had turned a sour yellow and begun to peel in places. On one staircase, Caz nearly fell because the carpet had come away from the floor. Having long ago given up trying to escape, the desiccated bodies of dead insects lay abandoned and unclassified on windowsills.

At the top of the house they reached a corridor that was different. The deep-pile nut-brown carpet was fitted and the walls freshly painted. Someone had dusted and vacuumed recently.

'This is where Lacy lives, it's the only bit that's really kept up,' explained Ronnie.

Stopping outside a plain white door, Ronnie removed his shoes and signalled for Caz to do the same. Holding his shoes in one hand, he gently turned the doorknob.

Apart from a metal chest and a black lacquer screen, there was no other furniture in the room. There was something peculiar about the smooth white walls and it took Caz awhile to realize that the room had no windows. Ronnie shut the door. The floor was made out of woven straw.

'*Tatami*,' Ronnie explained.

Six sheathed swords were mounted on one wall alongside a creepy white mask. A swollen black grin mocked them, while two empty eye sockets locked onto Caz and followed her as she moved about the room.

'That's an *oni*, a Japanese demon. Legend says if you put the mask on, you can see into the past. Here,' Ronnie picked up the mask. 'Why don't you try it?'

He held the sinister thing out to her.

'Scared? Okay, I'll go first.' Ronnie was just about to put the mask on when they heard a door slam nearby.

'Fuck,' muttered Ronnie. 'Over there.' He pointed out a hiding place.

They heard footsteps approaching as they cowered behind the screen. The noise got closer, and Caz could see the mask back on the wall grinning toothlessly at her through a crack in the screen. She felt as if the noise of her own heartbeats would be loud enough for Ronnie to hear. Finally, the footsteps faded. They waited for a minute or two before snatching up their shoes and fleeing the room, thudding down the stairs till they arrived back at the picture gallery, sliding along the polished floor in their socks.

'Good to see you've made yourself at home.'

They skidded to a halt in front of Lord Lacy.

'We were in the insect room,' Ronnie explained pre-emptively.

'The insect room, hmmm.' Lacy drew close enough for Caz to see the blue vein on his temple pulse.

'How apt, I was just reminded of a scene from *Lord of the Flies* when you came bowling down the corridor.'

Caz caught a whiff of something rotten on Lacy's breath just before he drew away and back up to his full height.

'Speaking of literature, have you had time to look at the Mishima, Ronnie?'

'I'm nearly finished.'

'But are you enjoying it?'

Ronnie blushed.

'It's a bit strange.'

'Strange, hmmm.' Lacy stared down at Ronnie who squirmed under his gaze.

He inspected them as if they were an interesting species of insect themselves.

'Is your mother about?' Lacy asked Caz.

'Rosie's here, but mum is back in the van.' Her own voice

sounded distant.

'Meditating,' added Ronnie.

'Meditating, interesting, we shall have to have a chat about that. So how are you finding the house, hmmm?' Lacy bent down again, his face looming above Caz.

'Fine I suppose, Chris might be back by the weekend, then we'll probably be off.'

'Hmmm, yes. We'll all have to meet up before then. How about dinner tonight, say seven o'clock?'

Caz didn't respond, but instead moved a step back. She couldn't stand having Lacy up in her face like that.

CHAPTER SEVEN

That afternoon Chris jangled up the driveway and clattered through their front door.

'Red gave me a lift up. Was happy to oblige. One less hairy body squished into his lounge. Dropped me off on the road, but it took me a good while to find this gaff. Still, not a bad little pied-a-terre you've set yourself up with ladies. All amenities sorted and what not. Tell you what, I'm half dead from the eye watering odours of stinky feet and man farts. If it wasn't the smell that done for me, it was the constant nattering. He's sound that Red, but he don't half go on about politics. Bit of a case of all mouth and no trousers though, judging by the actual action he's seen down in sleepy Trumpton. Anyhow, you fragrant ladies is a sight for sore eyes.'

He gave Tink a cuddle and a wet kiss, before passing her the soggy spliff he'd been puffing on.

'Where's the van?' asked Tink.

'Cops have still got it. The standoff continues, going back there at high noon. But never mind that for now, guess who's on the news tonight!'

Rosie, guzzling away at her thumb, regarded him with limpid blue eyes.

'Gonna be on the 6 o'clock news, thought we could all watch it together.'

'So we're still stuck out here then? You could have brought us down some food. There isn't a shop for miles.' Tink pointedly eyed Chris' bag full of cans of cider.

'Mum, I told you, Mrs Dixon gave us a bag of food earlier,' Caz said, looking up from the book she'd been attempting to read.

'Tidy, nice one. Then we don't have to worry. So, where's the telly then?'

'Hate to burst your bubble, but we don't have a telly here,' pointed out Tink.

'You're kidding!'

As if the weight of this disappointment were too much to bear, Chris dumped the cans on the table and plonked himself heavily down on the sofa next to Caz.

'What're we gonna do Caz?'

'You hate telly,' she reminded him.

'I know. We can watch it down the village pub with the local yokels. Might get a bit aggro though,' he ruminated.

Caz shifted further away from his potent aura of BO and stale cider.

'We've been invited up to dinner from seven at his Lordship's place,' said Tink.

'Trying to put the moves on while I was away, was he? In that case, I reckon we could cheekily rock up there a bit earlier and ask if he minds us using his telly,' said Chris.

******

At around half five they all trooped off to the house. The evening sun cast long skeletal shadows on the lawn behind them. Chris had been talking non-stop, telling them all about meeting the news crew, but as they mounted the steps and came to a halt underneath the frowning stone awning of the main entrance, he fell silent. Caz noticed that even though he hadn't dressed up, he wasn't cradling a can like usual.

Lacy had dressed down in brand new jeans and a freshly-ironed polo shirt. The starched white fabric brought out queasy yellow and green tones in his pallid complexion and the sight of

Chris standing on his doorstep with his bog brush mess of curls made Lacy look even worse for wear. The thumb set to work, this time stroking his index finger, so it looked as if he were counting out invisible banknotes, assuring himself that his fortune remained intact.

Chris seized these distressed digits and pumped them hard, sticking his oar right in and addressing Lacy with a deferential air that bordered on parody.

'Lord Lacy I presume. Apologies for our sudden arrival ahead of schedule, but we're here cap in hand so to speak to impose again upon your generosity and ask if we might have the use of your telly, only I'm on the news at six see and I wouldn't mind having a gander.'

Lacy's hand was released and now flopped half dead at his side, resting immobile for a moment before spasming.

'You must be Chris,' he said, looking stunned.

'Right you are and let me say right off the bat that I appreciate you looking after the misses and the little ones. Never had this kind of bother before, really, I'm forever in your debt so to speak. Though of course here I am being cheeky and asking another favour...'

'Of course, of course, come in. It's no trouble at all. I'm afraid the room where I keep the TV is a total pigsty though. It's something of a private den you see.'

He herded them into a room at back of the house. Stacks of paper and boxes cluttered every available surface, so that even after they'd picked their way through to the table, they couldn't sit down on the chairs.

'Do you mind if I...' Lacy said, taking a stack of files out of Caz's hands and moving them to another spot.

'Believe it or not, there's a system. A method to the madness,' Lacy explained.

They said nothing.

'Been cataloguing everything in the house. Deciding what goes under the hammer. A rather overwhelming task.'

Chris flipped the lid of a box and peered inside.

'Some tasty knickknacks you've got here Lord Lacy.'

'Please, call me Rupert.'

Lacy switched on the TV. The news wasn't on yet. He checked his watch, thumb drumming against his wrist. Caz moved her chair closer, she rarely got to watch Neighbours and always felt left out when her friends talked about Scott and Charlene.

'It looks like we've got ten minutes or so. Erm.' Lacy looked over at Chris who was now manhandling an ornate plate with an acquisitive eye.

'Erm, if you wouldn't mind. That plate, it's rather delicate.'

'No worries Rupert. Whoa there.' Chris pretended to drop the plate before swooping his hand back up to save it from destruction.

Lacy's face twisted in an agonized grin.

'If you were busy doing something, don't let us keep you,' said Tink, sweetly.

'No, no, I er, I'm interested myself in watching.' He hesitated before adding. 'I don't suppose you'd like some drinks?'

'A beer would go down a treat,' said Chris.

'Lemon squash,' simpered Rosie.

He walked backwards toward the door, scared to take his eyes off them.

'I'll just tell Mrs Dixon. Won't be a moment,' he said before dashing off down the corridor.

'Thinks I'm going to nick something,' said Chris.

Tink didn't laugh.

'Can you shut up? I'd like to watch Neighbours for once,' said Caz.

Lacy was back in time for the start of the news, carrying squash and a few dainty bottles of French beer on a tray. He stood after serving them, like a nervous butler.

Bong. 'The UN security council has unanimously condemned Iraq's invasion of Kuwait, paving the way for military action.' *Bong.* 'French workers begin work on the Channel Tunnel ahead of schedule.' *Bong.* 'And a quiet town in the Cotswolds becomes the focal point of tensions between the so-called new-age-traveller movement and the police,' the announcer read.

Chris and Tink cheered the last item.

Chris stood up to lower the sound when the newscaster segued into the headline news.

'I don't think we need hear that other rubbish, do you? Just a bit of propaganda from the man.' He flipped the metal lid off his beer and drank most of it down in one swig, burping noisily afterwards.

'I'm sorry, *the man*?' enquired Lacy.

'You know, the man in power. This is all about oil, high finance, nobody really gives a toss about those poor Kurds.'

'You make a compelling argument,' said Lacy, smiling.

'Yeah, right, that's the man, he uses the police, the army for his own agenda and brainwashes you through the telly to believe that it's all to help out the little people. He fucks everyone, then insists that they have a smile on their face while they're getting shafted. What we're trying to do see, is stick it to the man. He doesn't want anyone having fun, anyone being free. He's trying to crack down on our rights. You ever hear of the Battle of the Beanfield?' Chris was overly animated, talking too fast.

'Give it a rest will you,' said Tink.

'Just let me tell Mr Lacy, I apologize, Rupert, this one thing. Our friend right, Baz, right, he 'aint been right since. Police went around smashing in windows, beating people about the head and like they was totally unprovoked,' Chris said, continuing to go off on one.

Tink sighed and cuddled Rosie tight.

'Mum, you're squishing me,' she complained.

'Shh, it's on,' Chris said, turning the volume up. They all turned to watch the TV.

'A group of protesters have pitched camp outside a police station in Barchester.' The camera panned over the crowd of protesters. Suddenly Baz's shattered face filled the screen, grimacing like a gargoyle as he took a chug on a big plastic bottle of cider.

'The group, who say they are "new age travellers," is demanding that the police return their vans and sound system after the equipment was confiscated at a so called "free party" last weekend. Sergeant Barry Winter, issued the following statement to the press.'

The camera focused a little too closely in on the stolid face of the policeman.

'We are holding equipment owned by the group known as Fractal Fracas while we investigate serious accusations of trespassing and breach of the peace. We understand that on August the fourth the group held an illegal party on private land.'

The camera cut to a picture of a farmer standing by a fence. 'Farmer John Boyle's field lies adjacent to the site of the party.' The farmer, a podgy man in wellies and a Barbour jacket was shown walking through a field of sheep. This sequence was followed by a shot of him standing next to a fence.

'They come down on Saturday in that field over there. Lots of them had dogs running wild, those dogs come through here and started worrying the sheep. It aint right, you can't let dogs loose like that on other people's land. Sides that land is private property, I don't think they got permission from nobody to be there.'

'The travellers are defiant, citing their right to roam.'

Chris came onscreen. He looked different, thinner. The TV had magnified the signature squiggle of broken veins across the bridge of his nose. His gestures were overblown as if he were attempting to conduct a rebellious orchestra.

'What we're doing right, is an essential thing for the community, for England. We don't believe in private property, we all ought to share. What's wrong with people getting together for a bit of a dance, right? That's what we want to know.'

'Would you say you were an anarchist?' the reporter asked.

Chris paused, invisible baton raised, then brought his hand down. He smirked at the camera and then looked back at the reporter.

'You could well say that, in that I believe in our basic right to party anywhere and the right for people to govern themselves.'

They cut to a shot of Barchester High Street.

'Residents of Barchester seemed divided on the subject.'

An old lady appeared onscreen.

'It's all a bit of fun, isn't it,' she said with a smile.

'Don't you think it creates a disturbance?' enquired the journalist.

'In the middle of a field? How ridiculous. Dragging them into town, now that's created a disturbance. Don't think Barchester's been this lively in years.'

Chris whooped. 'She's that old lady who gave us the French Fancies!'

'They're all a bunch of dole scroungers, aint they? Think they're entitled. Lazy sods. If they had a job to go to, they'd make themselves useful. Wouldn't be causing trouble like this,' a man shouted into the camera, the colour of his red face matching his heated words.

Even Lacy laughed along with them at this part.

The news moved on to the Channel Tunnel and Chris stood up and switched it off, faced them with his arms folded.

'Splendid stuff.' Lacy applauded Chris politely. 'So how long is this stand-off going to last?'

'Don't know, hope we get our stuff back soon, there's the Big Field at Tipton to go to this weekend. Don't want to miss it. Think they're holding our gear on purpose, so we won't get our sound system down there. All this stuff about the sheep is bollocks.'

'You're free to stay until you get your van back,' said Lacy.

'Cheers mate, appreciate it. We want to be off though, no offence.' Chris sniffed.

'None taken. But I think you're also secretly enjoying all this?'

'All wot?'

'The media circus, the conflict with the police. You certainly seemed to be enjoying the spotlight.'

'I don't pretend that I'm immune to the lure of celebrity.' Chris winked at Tink, who chuckled.

'But are you right? You said that you're doing this for the community, but what about the farmer whose sheep were bothered by the dogs. I'm just playing devil's advocate here.' Lacy held his hands up to show he wasn't about to stick the knife in. 'Personally, I don't mind you using that field, but the farmer next door, he makes his livelihood off the land.'

'Our dogs were all tied up, we don't let them run wild. Said before, that's just some bullshit they cooked up to keep our gear.'

Caz knew otherwise, a few dogs were always running loose at the parties.

'Let's say that's true, what about the litter? Bill said that there was a load of rubbish left behind.'

'We'd have cleared up, but no one gave us the chance, we got hauled off to the nick didn't we. That field of yours. What do you do with it, if you don't mind my asking?'

'Sometimes my estate manager rents it out to farmers as pasture,' said Lacy.

'And why do you have it? Because your great, great, great, great, great, great grandfather was a nasty violent bastard and took it by force.'

'More like he was a nasty violent bastard in France and the king gave him it as a reward, but you're on the right track.'

'But you're not doing nothing with it, so we just took it for the night, peaceful like. I'm no saint but think I'm a bit more civilized than that old ancestor of yours.'

'Most definitely, but if we all went around acting on our instincts and doing what we wanted, wouldn't the world be a very difficult place to live in? I'd like nothing better than to ride my sports car over the speed limit down these charming little lanes, but I'd be endangering the people around me. Fortunately, the law prevents me from doing so.'

'But people, when they're given freedom, show themselves to be basically decent. We all look out for one another. A party isn't going to hurt anyone, it's just going to make people feel better,' said Chris.

'People are basically good?'

'That's right.'

'I beg to differ. Remember that nasty bastard who was my ancestor? We're all like him underneath, avaricious, violent, out for ourselves, it's just the veneer of civilization that makes it seem otherwise.'

'Speak for yourself, M'Lord. As a member of the working classes, I don't carry that burden around.'

'Charming though you are, I think underneath it all, you're no better, it's just that your ancestors were probably not quite as efficient at cutting throats as mine.'

'They was too busy working themselves to death in the coal mines, or toiling the land. I'll tell you something for nothing.' Chris waved his fresh beer bottle at Lacy, not aware that it was liable to spill.

Tink cut in, 'Okay, cut the working-class hero act. Sorry Mr Lacy, I think celebrity has gone to his head.'

'Not at all, I love a lively debate. But how about continuing this over a nice bit of supper? I'm afraid it's a bit of a trek up to my digs, this is more of a workspace.' He paused and looked around him, as if he were taking in the disorder for the first time.

******

Lacy led them up the stairs, Rosie close on his heels and Caz just behind. At the top, as he waited for Chris and Tink to catch up, Rosie sidled up to him and took his hand.

'Looks like I've got to cut down on me fags,' Chris wheezed.

'Nearly there, only one more flight. The house is so stuffy, especially in this heat, I thought we'd all feel more comfortable up here,' said Lacy, leading them up a narrow flight of stairs.

They emerged out onto a square turret.

'This is my own little floating world.'

A large Persian rug was spread out on the rooftop, on top of which was a wicker pannier, a silver bucket, a bunch of throw cushions and an old wind-up gramophone. The heat of the day rose up through the tar beneath their feet. From the battlements they could see the woods spread out below, glowing faintly in the dying sunlight. Chris whistled; a sound that made Caz think of an arrow shooting off into distance. As if startled by this imaginary projectile, a flock of birds flew out of the trees.

Caz scratched her fingers along the brick, checking that this soft dreamlike scene still had life's usual rough edges. The stone gently grazed her fingertips leaving behind silvery particles that sparkled in the last rays of sunlight.

The noise of a cork being popped made them turn towards the picnic spread.

'I think this calls for a bit of fizz. I've got Veuve Clicquot for the adults and lemonade for the little ones.' He held up a bottle in one hand and a couple of long-stemmed glasses for Tink and Chris in the other. 'I hope you don't mind, but no shoes on these rugs, they're rather valuable.'

'Just as long as you don't mind my holey toes.' Chris shrugged off his army boots and grasped one of the flutes.

Lacy charged their glasses and then presented the girls with slender plastic glasses of the same design, which he filled with posh lemonade from a clear glass bottle.

'I propose a toast to mid-summer,' declared Lacy.

'To mid-summer,' they echoed, clinking glasses before settling down on the rug.

Rosie sat close to Lacy on an emerald green cushion. Every time he spoke, she turned to him and watched him open mouthed, twirling her hair coquettishly.

'We should have some music. I'm afraid my record collection is rather fusty though. It's mostly all classical.' Lacy popped open the clasp of a leather record case and held it out for Chris' inspection.

'Let's have a gander.' Chris began to flip through the records, assuming an expert air by occasionally lifting a disk and staring at it with one eye closed.

'I don't think he's got any techno, love,' said Tink. 'Give it here.'

Tink sat cross legged and began to carefully examine the box, finally extracting a record and handing it over to Lacy.

'The Magic Flute, wonderful, it's been years since I listened to this,' said Lacy.

'Me too. Thought the kids might like it,' said Tink.

Lacy put the record on. The music began, a pompous fanfare that hung heavy in the air. Lacy smirked at them. Holding up his long thin fingers, he pressed down emphatically on the horns, and then raised his fingers to dance higher in the air whipping up a light and frothy string passage.

'So, you like opera?' he asked Tink.

'Went to see this on a school trip years ago.' Tink was leaning back and looking up at the sky. She sighed with contentment. 'You've got a beautiful home.'

'That's very nice of you to say, but it's not really a home.' Lacy opened up a box of neatly made sandwiches.

'You own it don't you?' asked Chris, burping and holding out his glass for more champagne.

'Unfortunately, yes. But the damned place haemorrhages money. This roof for instance, I just had to have it resurfaced. Flat roofs are wonderfully romantic, but you pay through the nose for them. The whole place is falling apart at the seams.'

'Don't tell me you're strapped for cash,' said Chris.

'The family coffers are running dry and, quite frankly, I'm thinking of selling the bloody place to the National Trust.'

'That's sad,' said Rosie.

'Not really, it's far sadder living in this great pile all by yourself.'

Rosie stood up and patted him on his shoulder. He glanced up at her in surprise.

'Sorry. She's a bit over-affectionate. She's forever latching onto strangers,' said Tink.

'That's quite alright, it's sweet,' Lacy said.

He turned away for a moment and when he looked back, Caz noticed that the whites of his eyes looked red, vampiric. He sat unnaturally straight, with his heels tucked up underneath him, lifted the champagne flute and looked into the trails of bubbles flowing upwards.

'From my perspective, your life seems almost blissfully weightless. Unfettered by society's rules, you're free to come and go as you please.'

'It's not too shabby, I must admit. Course we're only on the move during summer, this bloody miserable climate aint much good in winter,' Chris said. 'Tried living in the van one time during winter and ended up going to the hospital with pneumonia, didn't I? See the problem is, you get a burner going, get all snug and cosy, a few cans of brew to settle you down for the night and nod off. Before you know it, you wake up freezing and your sleeping bag's soaked through. Thought I'd pissed myself the first time it happened. It's the condensation see, while you've been sleeping, the air outside is getting chilly, your breath starts steaming up the place, so all these little droplets right, they collect on the van roof. Then what do you think happens? They turn into icicles, that's what. Once the sun comes up, those icicles melt, don't they and you get woken up with a freezing cold shower. I was laid up in hospital for more than a month after that little experiment.' Chris extracted his baccy tin. 'Mind if I smoke?'

'Be my guest, no ashtray I'm afraid, but you can pop the ash on the roof. So, what on earth do you do in winter?'

Chris opened up his tin and began rolling a fag. He left the lid off, displaying a fat bag of weed tucked inside. Tink leaned over and replaced the lid, glancing at Lacy to see if he'd noticed.

'Find a nice warm squat and hole up till spring, that's what. Fact is, that's where Tink and me have been staying haven't we babe?' He leaned over and gave Tink a kiss on the cheek. 'You know Kentish Town? Just north of Camden, it's a place called Rainbow Retreat, right by the station, used to be a town hall, but it'd been empty for donkey's, so it got squatted. People there is pretty decent, it's not filled with junkies and wot not, just a bunch of sound people, a lot of them is quite political.' He sucked on his fag.

'How did you two meet then?' asked Lacy.

'She'd come down to Whirl-Y-Gig at Shoreditch Town Hall and I'd been DJing and we hit it off. The great thing about this party right is that you can bring your kids, so right away, I gets to meet these little beauties. It's absolutely brilliant, right, at the end of the night they get this old parachute, made of silk, beautiful thing, it belonged to someone's granddad who'd been a paratrooper in the war. Anyway, they get this parachute and drop it over the crowd, and everyone at the edges, which is usually adults, grabs a bit of cloth. The kids sit in the middle. Rosie, she loves it. You tell him Rosie.'

'It's a big cloth and we sit under and it's like being under the sea,' said Rosie, dreamily.

'We met through this little one.' Chris ruffled Rosie's soft blonde hair and she giggled.

'This cutie was throwing balloons at me, then I find out that her mum wasn't too shabby neither.'

Chris leaned over and gave Tink a cuddle.

'There was a room free at the squat and they moved in.'

Chris leaned back, looking satisfied with himself. Tink began to bite the skin off around her nails.

'Was that alright? Living in a squat with children?'

'It's safe, like Chris says, it wasn't filled with junkies or anything. People were really sorted, there was this guy from Berlin called Rafi right, actually he was born in Brazil, but he'd been living in Berlin. You know the Germans, they're well organized, so he made us a garden on the roof, fitted locks, painted these awesome murals on the walls. Most people there were pretty artistic, so everywhere was decorated with stencils and that. It's pretty amazing. They all loved the kids.'

Caz noticed her mum hadn't mentioned the rat problem. The others had thought it funny that a brood of baby rats had shot across the bathroom when she'd been on the loo. Nor the fact that they'd had to put bubble wrap over the windows and newspapers under their beds to keep out the cold.

They polished off a plate of smoked salmon sandwiches followed by slices of cold ham, wiping off greasy fingers with starched white napkins, before they got stuck into the cheeses, scattering cracker crumbs all over the place. For dessert, they had chocolate covered profiteroles that exploded with fresh cream, followed by fresh strawberries. They finished up just as the music ended, plastic plates scattered with the rinds of cheeses and starred green strawberry stems.

It was beginning to get dark and candlelight, coming from paper lanterns placed around the edges of the large Persian rug, gently lapped over its patterned weave. The needle picked up dead static and Chris' lighter caught, licking his battered face with a fiery orange flame.

Lacy put on another record. A piano performance recorded sometime in the distant past. Despite the hiss and crackle of accumulated dust, the notes, like the stars that were beginning to appear in the darkening sky, though faint, twinkled, cool and distant.

'The underwater cathedral, Debussy,' explained Lacy.

Rosie lay asleep at his side.

'So, Chris, I take it you're not a fan of classical music then?' Lacy asked.

'No no, lovely, peaches and cream, it's good for a sophisticated get together like this. But I like my music a bit on the dark and dirty side. A nice bit of grimy techno, like mainlining a chocolate gateau if you know what I mean.' He reached over and recharged his glass, polishing off the bottle of white wine they'd had with their dinner and looking hopefully over at Lacy to see if there might be any chance another bottle would materialize.

'I'm afraid I don't, dance music seems to have bypassed Barchester up till now. Besides, it's hardly dignified at my age to be jerking this stiff old carcass across a dance floor.'

'That stiffness aint rigor mortis setting in, it's your bloody dignity. You're not dead yet, though judging by the colour on you, you could be,' said Chris

Lacy held out a white hand and considered it.

'What you need is a nice boogie. Listen, me and Tink was thinking of having a bit of a get together at the house once the van's been freed up. That is, if you've no objections.' Chris concealed a burp at the end of this sentence with a cupped hand, a concession to the elevated society he currently found himself in.

'A party? Well, you have rather sprung this on me.'

'When's the last time you really enjoyed yourself? How old are you then Rupert, if you don't mind me asking?' asked Chris.

'Just gone 42.'

'So, you're not cashing in your pension yet then? How come you're mouldering away here in this dusty place? Come on, just an informal little do, shake you up a bit.'

'I suppose it would be okay, as long as you don't carry on too late and keep the numbers down.'

'That would be blinding. I'll make sure there's plenty of brew and maybe we'll get you dancing.'

Caz stood up and walked away over towards the battlements. She looked down at the fountain. The central figures were bone white and ghostly: a muscular bloke on an equally muscular horse was about to plunge a spear into the heart of a sea monster that writhed at the horse's feet. A lady in as much a state of undress as distress lay nearby helplessly watching on. Ornamental fish gasped thirstily at its edges, their eyes bulging in a state of constant panic, mouths gormlessly open. The fountain was bone dry and weeds grew along cracks in its concrete bowl.

The full moon shone brightly over the treetops. Without the wind rustling their leaves, the great old oaks fell silent. Caz gripped the stone wall in front of her. Something flickered at the edge of her vision and her chest lurched. When she scanned the scene to reassure herself that nothing had changed, she caught sight of their room visible over the treetops. Had they left the light on? It had still been light outside when they'd left.

A shadow fluttered across the wall. She felt giddy, as if someone had pushed her at the edge of a cliff top and then pulled her back again.

It's just a moth, she told herself.

******

They finally began to wend their way home around 11. Rosie, who'd fallen asleep and had to be roused, was blearily following Chris and Tink's wavering path across the lawn. Tink was holding Chris up a little and laughing as he whispered impressions of the hapless Lacy into her ear.

'Welcome to one's floating world, one likes to sit up here with a shotgun and pick off the plebs when one is feeling lonesome. Though occasionally if a country lass takes one's fancy, one invites them up for a roll around on one's Persian rug.'

A full moon rose behind them, bright enough to print soft slanted shadows on the turf in front of them; inky figures that mimicked their every move. Caz strode ahead trying to stamp out the dark stain that pooled at her feet, but it continued to glide in front of her, just out of reach. She remembered the shadow she'd seen flitting across their window and slowed as she approached the tree line. A faint trickle of moonlight seeped into the edges of the wood but wasn't able to penetrate the murky depths beyond. The trees sighed, moved by a cool light breeze.

'Lord, I just realized, we haven't brought a torch,' exclaimed Tink, arriving at her side.

'S'alright, I'll use my lighter won't I,' said Chris manfully.

He sparked up and began to shuffle forward through the trees. They hung close behind, holding onto each other as they inched down the narrow path, shrinking away as branches clawed at their limbs. After a few steps, Chris turned round and held the flickering flame up to his face.

'You stay close kiddies, there be tales of beasties afoot in these woods after dark.'

Tink slapped him. 'Don't scare the kids.'

Chris laughed and walked forward. Something shuffled in the bushes just as the lighter blew out and Caz thought she caught a glimpse of something moving off among the trees.

'Ow, fuck, it's red hot. Just wait a minute for it to cool down.'

Chris finally got the lighter going again and they picked up the pace, surfacing from the dark foliage into the familiar clearing. With the bulb in their bedroom up top glowing dimly, the house had the comforting look of a lighthouse. Rosie had simply left the light on.

Tink got the door open and switched on the downstairs lights. The house was as they'd left it. Rosie lay down on the sofa, curled up, plugged her thumb in her mouth and closed her eyes.

'Tuckered out, little thing,' Tink said, stroking Rosie's hair out of her eyes. 'Leave her down here tonight, eh? I'll just nip and get her a blanket. Chris and I will be in the trailer if you need us.'

After they left, Caz began to mount the stairs, the hairs on her arms standing on end as if the air held a static charge. She put her hand on the cold metal doorknob and listened, hearing only the clang of the trailer doors outside. She turned it slowly and threw the door open, putting her hand on the doorframe to steady herself. The missing rag doll lay on the bed regarding her coolly through its blue button eyes. With its slit black irises sewn over the plastic pupils and stitched red mouth curving upwards in a tight grin, the thing had a sinister look.

When Caz picked it up, its head fell backwards, limp. She rushed back downstairs and found a carrier bag in the kitchen, stuffing it inside. She didn't want to risk waking Rosie by going out to the bins, so found a chair and stuck it on top of the highest cupboard. From the ground you couldn't tell there was anything there, unless, of course, it decided to crawl out again in the middle of the night. She banished the thought and tried to be sensible. Rosie could have found the doll and put it on the bed herself, though it was strange she hadn't said anything. Even now she'd got rid of the doll, she still felt like there was someone crouching in some cranny, waiting to spring out at her. So she checked every single cupboard in the house to make sure there weren't any other nasty surprises waiting for her.

Freaked out to be by herself in the top room, it took her

ages to get to sleep after that and when she did nod off, the light still on, she dreamed she had put the Japanese mask on. She was in the insect room, peeping out through the eye sockets, the displays beginning to flicker, tiny insect wings fluttering ineffectually behind the glass. She went up to the glass and peered down at a struggling butterfly. Its torso writhed, trying to free itself of the pins that held it down. The moon-like mask, reflected back at her in the glass case, loomed over the reanimated bodies, grinning sadistically. She fled the room and came out in the corridor. The paintings had also seemed to come alive, but they were playing a game with her, widening their eyes or twitching their mouths just at the corners of her vision. She whirled around, trying to catch them out, until finally the pink lady opened her mouth and burst out laughing. Caz picked up the painting and flung it to the floor where it smashed, allowing the woman to worm her way out of the frame. Caz ran, pursued by this crawling spectre, until she reached the door to Lacy's sword room. A dark pool of blood was leaking out into the corridor below the door.

CHAPTER EIGHT

The air smelt of sun cream and burnt plastic. Caz sat out on the front step smooshing the contents of her ice pop with her fingers, before slurping up the bright blue syrup inside. Sweat trickled down from her armpits to the crook of her elbow. She wiggled her toes inside her vivid pink jellybean sandals to try to get some airflow going, but it was no use.

Inside, Tink sat naked at the kitchen table trying to thread a bead necklace. The plan was to sell some jewelry on the street next time they swung by a big town. Groaning from her hangover, she groped for the plant sprayer every five minutes, so she could cool herself down with a fine mist of water. Rosie sat beside her, breathing through her mouth while making a bracelet from defective beads.

Chris had left them stranded again, but it didn't matter. It was too hot to be going anywhere. Madonna was playing on the radio, Caz singing along under her breath. She checked herself. What would Ronnie think if he heard her singing? Worse, what would he make of Tink sat naked in the kitchen? They'd parted casually with a non-committal promise to see each other 'around', but were their paths really going to cross before Chris got his van back? Rosie shot past, interrupting her train of thought.

'God, you're SUCH a brat,' she shouted after her sister's retreating figure.

The molten air rippled in Rosie's wake. It was the hottest

day ever. She could practically hear her own skin sizzling. She ought to move into the shade... But inside the metal trailer she'd be roasted alive, and she wasn't keen on the idea of getting an eyeful of her mum's tits back in the house either.

Standing up, her temples throbbed, violent green and black spots pulsing in front of her eyes. She dragged her heavy limbs across the driveway. The feeling that had crept over her over the last few months – that sometimes made it hard to get out of bed, like the air had turned to treacle – was magnified to an almost unbearable degree. She walked through a buzzing cloud of insects and entered the woods.

Though it was cooler under the trees, dust from the path clung to her sweaty feet, scouring the skin trapped beneath the weave of her plastic sandals. She took them off, feeling the soft earth beneath her soles. An army of ants was marching across her path, and she bent down to watch them, prodding their hard little bodies with a stick. Unlike her, they had somewhere to go and something to do. She might have once been curious to see the colour of their innards, but instead she tossed the stick aside and stood up. That's when she noticed Rosie, head bowed, half concealed in a hollow to the left of the path. Caz crept closer, slowly, so she could get a look at what her sister was up to.

The breeze dropped and the trees fell silent. Rosie was kneeling in the dirt in front of a fallen tree and seemed to be praying. A hush descended, as if the forest was a restless animal momentarily soothed by Rosie's muttered incantations. Caz was rooted to the spot, afraid that if she moved, she'd give herself away. After a minute or so, the flutter of feathers whipping through the air above set the scene back in motion. The silence had only lasted a few seconds but made a deep impact on Caz, who felt she'd seen something she shouldn't have. Rosie raised her head and stood up, brushing dirt from her frock.

Caz darted out of sight behind a tree, heart pounding as she listened to her sister approaching. When she thought it was safe, she peeped out and caught sight of Rosie looking back, crystal blue eyes shining through the trees, then sweeping away as she turned and walked back to the round house.

She made for the hollow and found the fallen tree that Rosie had been kneeling in front of. An assortment of objects placed upon a bed of leaves gave the impression of a makeshift altar. Two stolen tea lights, a bunch of wildflowers, one of the cupcakes Rosie had made with Mrs Dixon the day before, the homemade bracelet, an unopened packet of refreshers and a little plastic green-haired gonk, all laid out in tribute.

CHAPTER NINE

Even after the sun had gone down, nights at the round house were hot and humid. It was difficult to sleep that particular night. As if she could sense something silently brooding in the woods beneath her window, waiting to pounce, Caz stayed wide awake until dawn. As soon as the birds began to screech outside, she went out cold, waking up concussed and bleary around 11. She sat up and stared at the twisted sheet she'd kicked off onto the floor.

A gunshot rang out, giving her a sickening start until she realized it was the exhaust from Chris' clapped-out van backfiring. Looking out the window she saw he'd brought along a battered VW camper and an old ambulance that clogged up the driveway.

Chris had been right, the Barchester police, sick of the heavy scene in front of their police station, had returned the vans, leaving them free to go to The Big Field at Tipton for the weekend. After tramping into the house to make use of the amenities, leaving nasty looking smudges round the tub she'd just cleaned and wiry pubes in the special cake of strawberry soap Caz hadn't had time to hide, the usual suspects – Baz, Mags, Ollie and Suze – sat outside the house on an assortment of rotting deckchairs and cracked plastic furniture, baking their leathery skin in a shrinking patch of sunlight.

As the afternoon progressed, the group shuffled up the driveway, trying to catch the last rays of sunlight that were slowly ebbing away. Occasionally a sweaty adult would break out of the circle to fish a can out of the paddling pool nearby. Supposedly a present for Caz and Rosie, now filled with twigs, grass and dead flies, they'd long since ceded use of it to the adults.

Suze, who had a soft spot for kids, had brought some cardboard boxes out for Rosie and suggested they have a crack at making a galactic fleet. With nothing better to do, Caz joined in. It was a good chance to sit and chat with Suze. Younger and, Caz thought, prettier than Tink, with sharp dark features and straight brown hair, Suze was always darting around nose to the ground, eyes twinkling, sniffing out mischief, like a squirrel hunting for acorns. Her hands were always scratching around for something to do, and she had a nasty habit of picking at fresh scabs or squeezing spots, even trying to squeeze one of Caz's once. In general, Caz considered her to be pretty sound, especially seeing as she would toss any clothes she'd 'got bored with' her way.

They spread themselves out on a blanket in the shade, decorating their ships with fistfuls of felt tip pens, while nearby, Suze's boyfriend, Ollie, strummed Space Oddity on his guitar. When the black and purple ran out, Rosie lost interest, leaving her box discarded by the tree line, after making a half-hearted expedition out to Alpha Centauri. But Suze continued to work on her craft, while Caz rolled over on her back and stared up at the sky, pebbles digging into her flesh through the woollen blanket.

'Tink says you made a friend at the manor,' Suze said, decorating the cockpit of her ship with a complicated set of dials and knobs.

'Ronnie? I only met him once, just a couple of days ago,' replied Caz non-committedly.

'So, what's he like then? Dishy?'

'He's alright, a bit posh, but his mum, the housekeeper, speaks like a proper yokel. "Ar, there be nasty travellers in these parts,"' she said, hoping to make Suze laugh.

'Upwardly mobile, is he? Bit like Chris here. You'd never

guess he was the product of a grammar school education, would you? Course he likes to go on about his communist dad and growing up on a council estate and all that, but he neglects to mention the scholarship he won to the posh school. Bright lad is our Chris, likes to hide that fact with a mockney accent.'

Above, fluttering leaves lapped at the edges of a circular patch of sky, framing a towering fat storm cloud. Gilded in golden sunlight the gloomy edifice seemed to press down on Caz. As it swelled in size, the air thickened. The dogs lay their heads down on the floor, ears drooping and eyebrows lifted quizzically.

Like the flies trapped in the paddling pool water, the group struggled against the weight of the humidity, waving their limbs around excitedly to the music, desperate to break free from the torpor of the muggy afternoon by drinking tinnies and smoking weed.

Chris, who'd being puffing wetly away at his accordion, looked up at the clouds and pronounced, 'Cumulonimbus, looks like we're in for a storm.'

Ollie, who was idly strumming his guitar, glanced warily at the sky.

'Nah, it'll clear up.'

'My geography A-level says otherwise mate,' replied Chris.

'Suze, fancy a glass of my magic potion?' said Tink, who'd sidled up nearby.

'Oh, don't mind if I do.' Suze laid down her spacecraft and took hold of the plastic cup.

'What's that?' asked Caz.

'A grown up's drink,' replied Tink.

'I'm nearly 14, can I have some? I've had a beer before, haven't I?'

Tink and Suze laughed at her.

'This is a bit more potent than beer sweetie. You want a few more years on you yet,' said Suze.

The ruby coloured drink Suze was holding shone enticingly in the cup.

Caz sat up and caught sight of Rosie heading off into the

trees with a plastic carrier bag in her hand.

'So, when are we going to meet his lordship then?' Suze asked.

'He ought to be rocking up some time soon. I casually mentioned to him that a few townies would be turning up later, so I reckon he'll be keen to make it quick. Seems he's none too popular with the locals. Suits us though, he'll be here early when things is nice and polite. After he's gone, we can really crank it up. Sweet as a dollop of Nutella,' Chris said, cracking open a can.

'Why don't the locals like him?' Caz asked.

'That's for me to know and you to ponder over young Caz.' Chris tapped his flushed nose with a tobacco-stained finger.

Irritated, Caz went off into the woods in search of Rosie. Restless eddies in the air briefly whipped up fallen leaves before letting them drop back onto the floor. The cackling of the gang rang out nearby and Caz flushed, wondering if Suze had sniffed out her crush and was now telling them all about it. She strode away, angry. After five minutes she realized she'd gone too far and retraced her steps, trying not to jump as something small scurried away through the undergrowth. The path to the hollow was narrower than she remembered, but she recognized an old sock she'd seen lying on the floor before; this was definitely the right way.

She didn't see Rosie until she drew nearer. Sat lower, cross legged, arranging more items on her little shrine. This time she ducked closer to the ground, as if she sensed she was being stalked. Caz watched as Rosie took Tink's lighter and tried to get the tea lights going. A good moment to make an entrance.

'Mum's going to kill you for stealing her lighter,' Caz said, stepping into view.

Rosie stopped, blushing hard at the realization she'd been found out.

Caz picked up a cup filled with juice.

'What's this? A teddy bear's picnic?'

Rosie shook her head.

Caz crouched closer to her sister.

'Listen, I won't tell if you let me in on the secret.'

Rosie squirmed and looked around to check they weren't being watched.

'It's for the little girl,' she breathed.

'Little girl?' Caz said.

'Shhh, you'll scare her away.'

'What little girl,' Caz whispered.

'The little girl that's lost in the woods. I'm going to find her and bring her home.'

A light breeze prickled Caz's skin and the distant noise of thunder rumbled above their heads. Someone was crashing through the trees towards them. They both looked up to see Lacy walking along the path to the round house. Rosie dropped the lighter and ran off to meet him.

'A welcoming party, how nice,' he said.

Rosie took his hand.

'Would you like to see our spaceships?'

'I certainly would,' he said, allowing himself to be led to the party.

'It's only me for now, but Ronnie says to tell you he'll pop down shortly,' Lacy said over his shoulder to Caz who had just caught up.

******

'Rupert mate, come over 'ere.' Chris staggered towards them and extended a welcoming hand to Lacy, slapping him on the shoulder with the other.

Keenly aware that he was being sized up, Lacy cast nervous glances around the group.

'You know Tink already, here's Baz who you might recognize off the news.'

'Alright mate, nice gaff you got here like,' Baz said, raising his tinny.

Cautious greetings were shared with the rest of the group and a deckchair was freed up for Lacy to sit on. They shuffled into a semi-circle around him and waited for him to speak as he flopped about, trying to sit upright.

'Is there anywhere I can pop these?' He took a six pack of Fosters out of a carrier bag.

'Nice one mate, I'll just pop them in our outdoor refrigerator cum spa, but might I suggest that before we crack these open, you partake of some of this ere punch that my lady, erm, well I can't say wife, what should I refer to you as my dear?' Chris asked Tink.

'Trouble and strife!' shouted Baz guffawing.

'How about light of my life?' countered Tink.

'Indeed, light of my life, this punch the light of my life has prepared for our delectation.'

'Erm, yes, that sounds lovely, punch, what a refreshing idea,' Lacy replied, looking unsure of himself.

'Refreshing indeed my dear chap. I predict it will completely perk you up,' said Chris.

Lacy handed the beers to Chris and leaned awkwardly back into the chair.

Caz slipped away from the group and followed Tink into the kitchen. Peeping in through the doorway she saw her mum take the punch bowl down from the top of the cabinets and slipped back out before she got spotted.

Tink handed Lacy his cup and sat down next to him, saving him from Baz who was garbling in his ear and spraying him with saliva in the process.

Ollie, who sensed that Baz was beginning to get a bit aggro, segued into a cheerful rendition of *Lovely Rita*.

'*When it gets dark I'll tow your heart away. Ahh ahhhh, ahhh, ahhhh. Rita!*' sang Suze, offering a crooked arm to Caz. Suddenly excited about the evening's possibilities, Caz took it and they skipped in a circle, arms linked.

Thunder rumbled overhead and the trees sighed thirstily as if they could sense an impending downpour. Lacy gulped down his drink.

'This really is delicious, I must compliment you,' he said to

Tink.

'Not a patch on the spread you put out for us though, now that was something,' said Chris.

'No, but honestly, what's in this, it's very refreshing.'

The others tittered and Lacy looked down at his knees, thumb ticking against the plastic glass. A few droplets of rain spotted the ground, releasing a musky scent of wet earth into the air.

'What's that you've got there girl?' Ollie said to Suze, who was returning from the woods.

Suze waved a leafy branch from side to side.

'I thought I'd get closer to nature.'

'Ah, the forest advances, like in Macbeth, come to destroy the hubris of man,' Lacy commented.

'You wot?' asked Baz, head wobbling round and unfocused eyes glinting with the threat of violence.

'We need more green, you're right Rupert mate, man's hubris needs to be vanquished,' laughed Chris, reaching back to snap off another branch, triggering a stampede into the woods to strip branches off trees, or snatch up wild flowers.

Rosie returned with a bunch of dandelions, fat stalks oozing gluey sap down her wrist.

'I crown you our midsummer night's queen,' said Suze, plucking a dandelion from Rosie's fingers and placing it behind her ear.

'Oooer, she's off.' Baz cocked a finger at Suze and delivered a knowing wink to the company.

Rosie giggled as Chris lifted her up onto a chair and they gathered round, bowing and waving fronds of leaves in benediction.

Suze began to sing. *In the woods there grew a tree, And a fine fine tree was he, And on that tree there was a limb, And on that limb there was a branch, And on that branch there was a nest, And in that nest there was an egg, And in that egg there was a bird, And from that bird a feather came, And of that feather was, A bed.*

They began to circle round Rosie, humming along to the

folk tune. *And on that bed there was a girl, And on that girl there was a man, And from that man there was a seed, And from that seed there was a boy, And from that boy there was a man, And for that man there was a grave, From that grave there grew, A tree, In the Summerisle, Summerisle, Summerisle, Summerisle wood, Summerisle wood.*

Above, the cloud frowned over the treetops and growled fiercely. As they felt the first drops of rain fall, they began to speed up. The folk dancing had devolved into a kind of rain dance. They hooted like Indians, tapping their mouths with their fingers. Caz dropped out of the circle and saw that Lacy was also standing at the edges, drumming his thigh with his thumb, eyes on Rosie, a strange smile fixed on his mouth.

It was as if they'd all fallen under the influence of whatever was lurking in the woods and were casting a primitive spell to help to bring it out into the open. They yelped and howled and the leaves rose and fell, shaking in their hands. The dogs began to bark. Rosie stood stock still with a serious expression on her face, even when the rain began to drench her to the bone and the group broke up, darting for cover inside the round house.

******

The yellow institutional light inside quickly curdled the atmosphere, and the adults began drinking more heavily to soften the sour effect. Some of them had brought the severed parts of the forest inside with them and branches lay discarded on the floor. Rosie sat up on the sideboard, breath clouding the window, nose against the glass, flesh flattened, not even flinching when a clap of thunder struck just above their heads.

'One elephant, two elephants, three elephants,' Suze and Caz counted, before they saw a flash of lighting flicker over the chairs outside.

'Is it just me, or is this room slowly revolving? Have you got an army of little imps in the basement operating some rusty old subterranean machinery?' said Suze, slumped on the sofa, t-shirt hiked up provocatively to reveal a pale little pot belly.

'To what porpoise, dear Suze?' asked Chris.

Suze looked over at him.

'Innit obvious? To do our bloody heads in!' she cackled.

'Let me get this straight, you believe that I have an army of magical creatures in my employ?' said Lacy.

'Exactly that,' she nodded. 'Quiet, can't you feel it? The tiniest movement? Shh, they're working the wheel. Can't you hear the cogs turning?'

Lacy looked around him. His face had a slight greenish tint.

'What do you think Rosie? Do you believe I'm commanding an army of dwarfs?'

Lacy addressed Rosie, who was staring out of the window at the driving rain.

'Imps!' corrected Suze.

Rosie, in a trance as usual, didn't reply. Caz counted ten elephants in her head before the next flash of lighting. The scene outside had darkened to an underwater shade of green, rain lashed the surface of the paddling pool and wind whipped the fabric of the deckchairs. A group of shadowy figures passed by the window and there was a knock at the door.

'That'll be Red and his mates,' Chris said, getting up.

'Don't open it, thems the imps!' Suze shouted, poking Caz with a sharp elbow.

Chris threw open the door to reveal a bedraggled group holding a plastic sheet over their heads. They dropped the sheet by the doorway and shuffled in. There were two men and one woman. With their hair running with water, they looked to Caz like a bunch of drowned rats. Red she recognized only because of his dyed hair. Chris introduced the other two as Pearl and Dominic. They looked eagerly at the travellers, some of whom they'd already met at the protest, pretending, but not succeeding, to appear casual. After introducing the kids and Tink, Chris gestured to Rupert.

'And this is our kind host, Lord Lacy, but he says we can call him Rupert.'

'Alright,' Red said, greeting Lacy with a cold nod.

The others remained silent, coolly looking at Lacy with undisguised disgust.

While everyone else was slumped against the furniture and walls, Lacy sat upright. With his legs crossed and fingers knitted tightly over one knee, he looked as if he were keeping himself under restraint. But there was a force welling up in him that caused his thumb to twirl, his legs to jump and head to twitch suddenly without warning.

'Would you all like some punch?' Tink asked the new arrivals.

'Magic, yeah, we heard from Chris about your punch,' Red said. 'We brought along some of the local cider too.'

The travellers made approving sounds and softened a little towards the newcomers, offering them space on the floor and a tiny perch for Red on the edge of the sofa. The punch arrived and they sat taking small sips.

'Whose is the VW?' Pearl asked, craning her neck round to look at the group.

'That's mine and Suze's,' said Ollie.

'It's really brilliant, I like the way you've painted it. I'm saving up for one myself, but I don't know where to get one.' Pearl had twisted round and was now kneeling in front of Suze and Ollie, looking up at them with wide eyes.

'Picked this one up through Exchange and Mart didn't we Suze, 400 squids.'

'Tidy,' said Pearl, nodding her head.

'So, you're all locals are you?' asked Suze.

'Dominic and Red are, but I came here for uni, never got it together to leave,' said Pearl.

'Like it here?' Suze asked.

'It's alright, once I get a van though, I'll be out of here. I like your boots, where did you get them?' said Pearl, eyes hungrily appraising Suze's outfit.

'Army shop down in Brixton.'

The sofa began to jiggle as Lacy's crossed legs bounced up

and down, he turned and looked over to Tink.

'Is it me, or is it rather airless in here? Perhaps it's being back in this place. I've always found it rather oppressive. But of course, it could just be the weather.' He trailed off, looking about himself frantically.

Chris, sat enthroned in the comfiest armchair, sipped his can and watched Lacy's obvious agitation with relish.

'Pity about the rain. I think some of us could do with a bit of a boogie,' Chris observed.

'You know I really am beginning to feel rather out of sorts, perhaps I ought to go home,' Lacy continued, still looking at Tink.

'You're not going anywhere in this rain,' replied Tink. 'Come on, why don't you come into the kitchen with me where it's nice and quiet?'

Lacy and Tink went into the kitchen and Caz followed. She hesitated in the doorway, watching Lacy as he gripped the counter, wobbling as if he were about to fall on the floor.

'Do you know I think I've completely forgotten how to be in a room full of people. It's been so long. Social skills are the opposite of riding a bicycle, more like learning a language, use it or lose it. You forget how to speak that language, can only remember fragments, the exchanges become fractured, misunderstandings accumulate,' said Lacy.

'People aren't meant to be alone, we're meant to spend time with each other. That's why I like this life, you're always with people. They get on your tits sometimes, of course, but it's never boring,' said Tink.

'It's like looking at yourself in a mirror too long, you can't see anything except your own flaws, you only really truly see yourself reflected in the eyes of others. Alone your flaws get magnified, you sicken of your own company.'

'Why don't you sit down and let me give you a massage?'

Lacy continued to grip the counter until Tink placed her hand on his arm and guided him into a chair.

'Have you ever had an Indian head massage?' asked Tink.

'I'm not too good with touching, with people touching me. I'm afraid I just freeze up. Actually, I'm feeling rather out of sorts. I really think I should go.'

Ignoring him, Tink began digging her fingers into his scalp, pushing his hair into his eyes as she did so. Chris crept up behind Caz to peep through the door too.

'Just close your eyes,' whispered Tink.

Lacy fell silent and shut his eyes, the rain pattered on the window and Tink looked up at her audience, shooed them away with one hand.

Back in the lounge Suze was kicking her heel against the couch. They all kept looking at the window straining for the rain to stop and release them outdoors.

Chris strode to the door and stuck his head out. 'It's only spitting, I reckon we could get set up. Better than us all stuck in this room frotting our seats bare with pent up energy.'

They all cheered, and the bustle began to set up the sound system. Van doors opened to disgorge bundles of snaking wire on the sodden ground near the sound system, while up above thin grey clouds moved fast through the darkening sky.

Chris' sound system, barely held together with duct tape, buzzed and crackled into life and the bass began to thump, kicking against Caz's rib cage till she thought her heart would burst under the pressure.

Incredibly, Rosie had crawled onto the vacated sofa and was now falling asleep. The adults stood about outside, tapping their feet a little uneasily. Suze and Ollie had decided to dive right in and were bobbing about, floating together on waves of purple and indigo sound. The others began to join in.

Tink and Lacy emerged from the house. Lacy looking dazed as the waves of noise washed over him. Tink took his hand and swayed from side to side in time to the music. Lacy swayed too, feet stumbling awkwardly over the complicated rhythms, looking as if he were about to trip and fall.

It was getting darker; yellow light from the round house sloshed weakly out from a window. White strobes and red and purple lights played across the shadowy figures of the lurching adults, suddenly illuminating gritted grins and bulging intent eyes.

Caz stood at the edges of the group, observing Lacy who was still standing beside Tink, gripping her tiny hand in his. He stood super straight, like he was balancing some invisible weighty tome on his head. All the others seemed unencumbered by comparison, hunched over their fags or cans, their drooping ape-like figures moved fluidly under the influence of booze and tunes.

Suddenly Lacy began to move, head jabbing forward, poise lost to the music. Unlike the others, his movements were staccato, like a cricket hopping around a field of corn. The others applauded and a rictus grin flashed on his face. Tink danced at his side, arms encased in ridiculous flowing Indian fabric. An oversized butterfly flapping up and down, she smiled at him dreamily as he jigged from foot to foot. Then she took his hands and tried to communicate the flow of the music to him.

It was then that Caz spotted Ronnie standing at the tree line, hands stuffed into his pockets, weight on one hip, the other leg bent forward, ready to disappear off into the woods if startled. He wore a private smile that indicated a disdain for the travellers, or for Lacy, or both.

She went over to fetch him, worried that Baz, who was stumbling dangerously close, might scare him away. He didn't seem to notice her approach, so Caz was forced to touch his slender bare arm to get his attention. He turned to face her.

'Hi!' she shouted in his ear. Whenever she got close to him, she'd lose her composure; what had been meant to be a casually friendly wave had turned into an over-enthusiastic gesture that reeked of desperation. He turned, brushing his fringe away and letting it fall raffishly again over his left eye.

He lifted a hand in greeting, Indian style, too cool to shout over the din. Caz pointed at his chest then mimed bringing a cup to her lips. He cocked his head, pretending for a moment to misunderstand her performance, so that she had to point to a can and mime drinking again. He shrugged and gave her a slight smile.

CHAPTER TEN

The moon shone silver, a curved blade cutting a sharp outline in a navy-blue bolt of sky. With the scent of sap filling their nostrils, Caz and Ronnie crossed the lawn, carrying a couple of cans they'd sneaked out of the paddling pool, their trainers wet from the damp grass. The figures in the fountain showed up stark white in the gathering gloom, features alive with emotion as if they were straining against their skin of stone. The teenagers sat down on the steps with their backs to the manor and opened the beers.

'Lowenbrau, not bad.' Ronnie examined his can. 'I usually drink Heineken, but beggars can't be choosers.'

'Usually? At home?'

'No, at school on Saturdays, there's an offie that serves my friend. We go to the river and meet up with the convent school girls. There's this garden no one knows about, actually it's the bishop's garden, but he never uses that house. We call it the secret garden. We sneak in and get drunk.'

'Oh,' said Caz, wondering if he liked any of those posh convent school girls.

'Someone almost always pukes in the bushes,' he added, warming to the subject. 'Thunderbirds usually does that to me, but I've never been sick yet on beer.'

'Right,' said Caz, gingerly sipping the beer.

'Bet you're used to stronger stuff. You ever do any acid?'

Caz shrugged, unwilling to let him know she'd never even

tried a spliff.

'Lacy's really straight. He thinks drugs are like the worst thing.'

'Don't be so sure,' replied Caz, glad she was wise to something he wasn't. 'He's off his tits now. My mum gave him some of her special punch. He was freaking out earlier.'

'Seriously! Did you drink some?'

'No way my mum would let me.'

'You could nick some.' Ronnie had turned his body towards her and was looking at her with real interest for once.

'It's not worth the hassle.' It was Caz's turn to feign bored sophistication, though she felt sure her cheeks were flushed.

'I'll do you a trade. You get hold of some punch and I'll let you in on Lacy's dark secret.'

******

Chris was at the decks, but she couldn't see Lacy or Tink. More people had arrived, and the crowd was getting into it. She skirted round the dancers, sticking to the shadows. Someone she'd never seen before swooped up to her and cawed at her like a crow, before gliding back off into the throng.

She slipped into the house unnoticed, tiptoeing past Rosie who was still asleep on the sofa, thumb plugged into her mouth, a trail of slime running down her chin. In the kitchen she got a chair to stand on so she could get the punch down from the cupboard. She filled up an empty tumbler, replaced the bowl, put a coat on over her arm to hide the cup and rushed outside. In the middle of the dancers, Suze and Ollie were throwing some weird shapes with their hands. Caz kept to the shadows before ducking into the trees.

'You only got one glass?' said Ronnie when she returned.

'It's okay, I don't want any.'

'Oh no no no, you can't trip alone, don't you know anything? You've got to take some too.'

'I can't take any more, it's almost gone.'

'We'll split it.' He grabbed the drink and downed half, made a face and wiped his mouth with his sleeve.

'Yummy.' He held the cup out to Caz. 'You have to drink now, or we won't come up at the same time.'

Caz took the cup and drank. After she'd finished, Ronnie said he had to go get something so he could properly tell the story and asked her to wait for him on the step.

Caz sat alone, her arms wrapped round herself, more for comfort than warmth. Her stomach seemed to be lurching in tandem with the bats that looped erratically above her head. As the last dregs of daylight drained away, the scene about her became grainy and indistinct.

Ronnie returned after ten minutes or so with a large leather-bound tome. He sat down close to Caz and balanced the album on his knees, beating out a drum roll with his fingers on its surface, before pausing dramatically and then slowly opening it up. A thin layer of tissue paper rippled in the breeze and Ronnie held it down with his fingertips, prolonging the revelation. He closed his eyes and took a deep breath.

'Five years ago, Upton Park was a completely different place. On the surface, of course, it's still the same.'

He drew aside the veil of tissue to reveal the first picture. Caz strained to make out the image through the gloom. It was a photo of Lord Lacy standing arm in arm with a blonde woman. Despite the intimate pose, there was something clenched about the way they stood. A strip of paper pinpointing the date had been tucked into a plastic slot beneath the image. *February 7, 1985.*

This album was nothing like the jumbled pile of Snappy Snap envelopes Caz's mum kept in a plastic carrier bag in their grandparents' attic. Nobody had posed properly for her family photos, they weren't arranged in order, and having never been classified, they could be rearranged to tell any kind of story, but not pinned down to one solid coherent history.

Tink had often talked about living in the moment to Caz. But living in the moment seemed to involve leaving a trail of confusion and half-truths in your wake; each member of the family swearing blind that this photo had been taken in Scarborough, not Shipton, and that was the day that Rosie had broken her tooth, not the day that Caz had fallen in the river.

'That's Lady Lacy. No one knows where she is now. After she left, Lord Lacy went to Japan. I suppose he wanted to get as far away from here as possible. That's why this whole place was shut up for three years.'

He turned the next page and lifted the tissue paper. Two children were posing on the exact same steps they were sitting on.

'I can't see,' whispered Caz.

Ronnie fished around in his pocket and produced a lighter. He sparked up and held the flame over the photo. A boy in a cowboy costume held a gun up to the camera, squinting as he took aim. Beside him, a little girl wearing an expensive looking Chinese dress stood with her hands on her hips, challenging the camera in her own way. Neither child smiled.

'Shit,' shouted Ronnie. The lighter flashed out and he shook his hand hissing with pain. 'It's fucking hot.'

Caz's heart was pounding as she stared at the darkened image.

'Anyone look familiar?' asked Ronnie.

'You were the cowboy.'

'Of course, but... Here, you try.' He handed her the lighter. 'Look at the girl.'

Caz waited for a minute before striking her thumb on the wheel. The flame flickered over the image of the girl. The expression was more focused, less dreamy, but the resemblance was clear.

'Rosie,' she whispered.

'Now do you understand why Rupert freaked out when he found your sister?'

'I'm freaking out a bit myself now. Who is she?'

'That's Sophie. Rupert's daughter.'

The controlled gaze of the girl in the photo came to life in the light of the flame. Caz snapped off the lighter and little spinning wheels of light, falling like snowflakes, filled her vision.

'I mean, that was Sophie. Nobody ever found her, so we can't be sure that she's not alive out there somewhere. That photo was taken five years ago. In a few weeks' time it'll be exactly five years since she vanished.'

Caz sat dazed, grasping the stone step for support. It was deadly silent, so that when her stomach gurgled, the noise was extra loud, making her cringe. To her horror she also realized that she felt like giggling.

'As you can imagine, having their child ripped away from them like that tore Rupert and Jenny apart. When he found Rosie, it was a shock. Like Sophie had stepped back into his life. He might have even thought she was Sophie. Ever wondered why he didn't call the police when she turned up? Of course, Sophie would be about your age now.'

The whole thing seemed so silly. It couldn't be real. Her heart was beating faster and faster as she tried to hold down the laughter bubbling up inside her gurgling tummy. She stood up and ran off towards the fountain. The grass was springy and seemed to give beneath her feet, making it hard to run, as if a thin layer of foam padding lay beneath. It took her an insanely long time to put any distance between herself and Ronnie. She placed her hand on the lip of the fountain's pool and turned to check he hadn't followed her. He was still sitting on the stone steps looking out at her. The distance between them and the burst of physical activity allowed Caz to breathe a little more freely, though the effort from the run made her sink to the floor.

Ronnie began to move towards her. The moon illuminated his pale face, one eye glittering, the other half hidden behind his dark fringe. He was smiling and holding out a hand to her. She couldn't move and sat nailed to the spot, as immobile as the stone figures behind her. Ronnie knelt by her side and placed a cool hand on her back.

'If you don't watch out, wolfy fire face will come and get you,' he whispered in her ear. She looked back at his smiling face, horrified. Ronnie began to laugh uncontrollably.

'Wow you should see your face, you so have the fear.'

That whole story had been a fabrication. She was angry, but the laughter she'd had inside her had to come out and she fell to the floor, helplessly convulsed by a fit of the giggles. Ronnie sat by her side and watched her writhing around.

'Sophie used to laugh like that. She'd go into fits and couldn't stop. In the end she'd be choking, not breathing properly.'

The laughter had seemed to twist up her insides, so when she stopped her guts were all knotted up. Caz stood up and frowned, turned, pressing her palms against the stone rim of the fountain, and stared at the figures: the warrior with the spear looked particularly intense as if his head was going to explode and cover them in plaster.

'That's Perseus, rescuing Andromeda over there from Poseidon's sea monster. The fountain used to work, made a noise like a tsunami, but while Lacy was in Japan it rusted up. Poor old sea monster is looking none too happy about it, don't you think?'

Still holding onto the stone lip of the fountain, Ronnie bent his knees, leaned back and looked up at the night sky.

'Whooo,' said Ronnie, hauling himself up and keeping his head back to take in the stars. 'You try this, it feels amazing.'

Caz got to her feet and looked up.

'No, you have to make the noise, do it with me,' Ronnie said.

'You need to say "whoo," and pull yourself up off the ground really fast and look at the stars.'

They lifted off the ground together, rushing for a brief moment upwards, fighting gravity, before dangling their bodies backwards. The knot inside Caz loosened each time she repeated the action, until she could breathe properly again without having to think about it.

'Can we go inside?' Caz asked.

'Lacy doesn't like me wandering around the house at night on my own.'

'Oh go on, he's at the party, he won't know,' she wheedled.

'Show me some precious objects. I want to see stuffed lions, Egyptian mummies, a chandelier.'

'Not sure we can stretch to an Egyptian mummy, but I do know where there's a rather lovely chandelier.'

'Done,' said Caz, surprising herself by jumping up and executing a short spin. When she moved, her body felt light, as if she'd come unstuck from the ground and might, with a big enough leap, go floating off into space. She danced up the steps and began pirouetting on the landing. Ronnie followed and opened up the huge door a crack, allowing Caz to skip through into the cool dark hall.

'It feels like Scooby Doo,' she whispered. 'Some ghost is going to pop up and try to frighten us away.' She placed a hand on Ronnie's shoulder. 'But don't worry, it's only a bad guy in a sheet.'

'The precious things are this way, Velma,' said Ronnie, leading her up the stairs to the second floor.

'Hey, who are you calling Velma,' she shouted, voice ricocheting off the hard stone floor.

'Shhh,' Ronnie whispered. 'My mum'll hear us.'

Creeping theatrically up the stairs, the planks of wood groaned beneath her feet and protested again when she lifted her weight off them. Ronnie held up his hand to halt her progress and demonstrated how to keep to the edges of the steps so as to not make a sound. At the top, instead of heading towards the picture gallery, he led her down a dimly lit corridor that plunged into the heart of the house.

The dark plum-coloured patterns on the wallpaper seemed to be slithering around at the edges of her vision, though when she stopped to examine them, they settled back down into a static arrangement of florid swirls and whorls. Something was still off, and it took her a moment to realize that this artificial flora was growing like moss through the wine-coloured walls. She touched it and pulled her hand away in surprise. The design was raised and bristled against her fingers.

'It's growing, like a plant,' she said. 'Feel it.'

'Haven't you ever seen flock wallpaper before?' Ronnie asked.

'Flock,' Caz echoed, thinking that it was a funny word.

She looked at it more carefully, almost touching the stuff with her nose. The leafy pattern seemed to wave before her eyes, buffeted by the gentlest of breezes.

'There's something in here that's a bit more interesting than wallpaper,' he said, easing open a door beside her.

Inside, the scent of varnish and dust scratched at the back of her throat. Ronnie fumbled for the light switch, flipping it to reveal grubby off-white walls sweeping up to a lofty ceiling, in the centre of which hung a tarnished chandelier. Even though a few bulbs had burnt out, it was bright enough to dazzle Caz and grand enough to put the confusion of random items below to shame. The once regal room had now become a dumping ground: a set of ski equipment piled up in one corner, a BBC computer on top of an antique desk, a box of silver spoons nestled in the seat of a large wicker chair and a glass cabinet stuffed in equal parts with objets d'art and junk.

Ronnie went over to the cabinet and picked up a box, carefully placing it on the floor in front of Caz. She sank to her knees.

'Seventeenth century from Turkey. A calligrapher's box.'

Tiny diamond-shaped pieces of tortoiseshell and mother of pearl fitted together in a geometric pattern that rippled in front of her eyes, the surface of the iridescent mother of pearl swarming with colour and the dark tortoise shell glowing amber.

'Can I touch it?' she asked.

'Go ahead.'

As her fingers traced the seams, she felt as if she were picking up tiny vibrations. Caz closed her eyes and held her hand over the ornate box, picking up a hum through her flesh.

A silver lock held the box shut.

'Do you have the key?' she asked.

'No, Rupert keeps that.'

She wondered what Lacy kept inside. His will? A dagger? A gun? Poison?

'Show me something else,' she demanded.

Ronnie executed a mock bow and turned back again to the cabinet, returning with a huge azure vase. Tiny fissures ran through its surface making Caz afraid to touch the glowing enamel in case it came apart in her hands.

'Does Lacy even use any of this stuff?' she asked.

It seemed wrong to her that such beautiful things were buried away in this dusty house. No one would ever use or even look at them.

'Do you think he deserves to have all this? Does he even appreciate it?' she added, thinking out loud.

'Of course he does. He's the one who told me about that box. We're cataloguing everything right now. He might lend some pieces out to a London museum.'

'It's not fair though, is it? Why should he have all this when other people hardly have anything?'

'Because he appreciates it, he was born to it and it's a collection that can only truly shine in a beautiful house like this.'

She didn't bother pointing out the obvious; that all the stuff in the room appeared to have been abandoned. Perhaps it had been because of Sophie's disappearance.

'Are you up yet? I'm not feeling much,' said Ronnie.

'I think so. Everything seems... Fizzy,' she said, looking up at a huge chandelier above their heads.

'I know what you mean, but I'm not really getting any visuals yet,' he said, looking at his hand.

'Visuals?'

'You know, hallucinations.'

She watched as pencil thin shards of light grew out of each bulb and intersected to form a kaleidoscopic swirl of fractured crystal, each ray gently expanding and contracting as if the chandelier were breathing in and out.

'It's like a flower of light,' she said.

'Very pretty,' he said, unmoved.

Ronnie got to his feet and wiped the dust off his trousers. 'Let's go exploring, we can check out the south wing, the part of the house that's been abandoned, look for your Scooby Doo ghosts.'

'Okay, just give me one more minute,' Caz said, still gripped by the wheeling light display.

'How about I go for a slash, and we leave when I get back?'

'Sure,' said Caz, unable to tear her eyes away from the light fitting.

When he left, she lay down on the floor just under the light, head propped up with a sheaf of yellowing papers. The more she looked at it, the more enchanted she became. Her mum said that material possessions weighed you down, but this was doing the opposite, it was singing to her, lifting her up. Now Ronnie had gone, the faint hum of vibrating crystal grew more distinct. When she closed her eyes and listened, the noise grew louder, she began to hum too, matching the tone. It was like communicating with some higher power.

When Ronnie opened the door again, the noise shut off and she jumped to her feet, caught a quick glimpse of herself in a nearby mirror and was shocked by what she saw. For the first time she had a vivid impression of who she was. As if she'd stepped outside herself; she examined her own reflection without shame. Took in the flush of red in her cheeks, the glowing amber hair and the large dark irises. Entranced she walked up to the cold glass and peered in.

'The room looks bigger on the other side,' she said.

He stood next to her and peered in, shrugged. Caz scanned the contents of the room through the glass, and span round to check it corresponded exactly with the layout behind her – a game she used to play as a child. Turning back, she wove her hands quickly through the air challenging her reflection to keep up, heart skipping slightly as she detected a minute delay in the movements of her doppelganger. She tried again and this time the blur of delayed motion left a trail behind it.

'Did you see that? Check it out, when I move my hands really fast, they go all see through,' she told Ronnie.

'Oh boy,' he said. 'So, are you ready for an adventure?'

He picked up a heavy black torch and started snapping the rubber button off and on again. Caz turned away from the mirror and followed him. As they stepped out into the corridor Caz had an odd feeling, like when your ears pop after coming down from a mountain. Suddenly things had returned to normal. The situation had snapped sharply back into focus, and she remembered she was in the manor with Ronnie, that he had just told her that Lord Lacy's little girl had gone missing five years earlier.

'Any visuals yet?' she asked.

He shrugged. 'Perhaps it was a dud batch.'

'I'm pretty high, I think,' she said.

'Probably psychosomatic,' he said.

'What do you mean?'

'It's all in your head, you think you're high because you think you took drugs, we probably didn't have enough to do much. You should have brought more.'

She looked around and wondered if that were true, things did seem to have returned to normal now. Ronnie walked quickly up ahead, impatient to get to the abandoned wing.

'Have you ever been there before?'

'Lots of times when I was little, I used to play hide and seek with Sophie, but since it got shut up, just the once. The wiring is fucked and Rupert is worried that we'll plunge the house into darkness and electrocute ourselves in the process if we flip any switches. I'll be in deep shit if mum finds out, so not a word, okay?'

He paused at a blank white door.

'This must be it,' thought Caz, heart beating a tom tom.

Ronnie turned the handle and pushed, opening the door. The torch from Ronnie's light barely penetrated the gloom. It was like standing on the edge of a deep coastal shelf. When Ronnie closed the door behind them, they were plunged into pitch black, the dense atmosphere roaring in Caz's ears. Ronnie switched the torch back on and traced the beam over a ream of wallpaper that had half peeled away from the plaster wall.

'Check out the mould.' He swept the light up to the blackened cornices. The spotted black growth crouched above them, as if it were waiting to scurry down and attack when they weren't looking.

Ronnie opened a door off to the left and jabbed his torch in the direction of a four-poster bed.

'George the fifth slept here once.'

It looked like a museum exhibit, except for the fact that the folds of the heavy burgundy curtains were clogged with dust.

'We should take a look in the nursery next. It's well creepy.' Ronnie shone the torch under his chin and laughed like a cartoon villain, then struck off deeper into the black.

It was then that Caz heard the singing.

'Did you hear that?' she whispered to Ronnie.

'What?' he said.

'Over there.' She pointed off into the gloom.

They fell silent and the singing continued.

'A little girl. You don't hear her?'

'Wow, sorry for doubting you, you're *really* high,'

They had been inching slowly towards the source of the noise and now stood at a doorway.

The girls are so pretty, I first set my eyes on sweet... sang the little girl.

Ronnie threw open the door and the singing stopped, Caz followed him into the room, not because she wanted to go, but because she was too terrified to stay out there alone. The torchlight danced over an empty room, boxes stacked on one side and an old rocking horse on the other. Caz took the torch and kept turning around, like a cat chasing its own tail, trying to find the little girl.

'No daddy, no!'

The scream seemed to come from just behind her. Caz took to her heels back down the corridor, the floor seeming to concertina out beneath her feet before she finally flung the door open out into the house. Not caring now about waking Ronnie's mum, she pounded down the corridor and thumped down the stairs before dashing off across the lawn.

Ronnie caught up with her, grabbing hold of her arm and holding her tightly, digging his fingers into her flesh, so that she fell onto the soft turf.

'Let go!' she shouted.

They struggled, staining their knees and elbows with grass and mud. She tried to pry his fingers from her arm, but it was useless and eventually she gave up, instead glaring down at her lap and shifting her body away from him.

'What's wrong?' he asked gently, fingers still clamped fast to her flesh.

'You didn't hear it?'

'Hear what?'

'I'm not going back there again. I want to go home.'

'But you can't leave like this, all freaked out.'

Caz refused to reply.

'Are you sure you weren't hearing things? I mean, right before, you said you were seeing some weird stuff in the mirror. Drugs can make you hear weird stuff as well you know. I think I'm starting to come up too now. You can't leave me alone like this. I didn't mean to scare you by taking you to the south wing. I thought it'd be fun. Come on, can't you stay? I wanted us to spend some time together before you leave.'

He let go of her arm and she rubbed the spot where his fingers had dug into her flesh but didn't move away. Down the hill excited screams could be heard above the heavy artillery attack of Chris' sound system.

'You need some music. That'll make you feel better,' said Ronnie.

'Not that,' said Caz.

'I've got my Walkman back at the house. Don't go anywhere, I'll fetch it.'

Without waiting for her to agree, he dashed off back to the house, leaving her there alone. There wasn't really anywhere she could go, the last thing she needed was to see all those morons head banging away to a barrage of electronic bleeps, but she wasn't about to go back to the manor. She was stuck out there in a kind of no man's land between two opposing worlds. She sat crouched, nervously glancing around the lawn to make sure nothing approached from either direction.

Barely able to bring herself to look at the house, she turned to the forest. The black mass of trees seemed to be boiling; a host of deformed faces bubbling to the surface, gaping mouths ready to consume anyone who entered. Caz looked at the grass instead and rocked back and forth for comfort. If she stared at anything for too long, it began to twitch and move, and that scream she'd heard echoed in her brain. It seemed like forever before Ronnie came racing towards her across the lawn. He crouched and put an arm over her shoulders.

'Sorry I had to leave you. It's funny, I almost forgot you were there. I was like washing my hands for ten minutes, the water felt great.'

Caz had tears in her eyes.

'Coming on pretty strong now,' he commiserated. 'Just remember it's not real, it's like a fairground ride, you're safe, locked in. I'm sorry I freaked you out earlier, really.'

The tight knot inside her uncurled slightly and she laced her fingers with his, allowed him to pop a headphone into her ear.

'This was one of my dad's old albums. It's Melanie. The quality is a bit dodgy, but I think you'll like it.'

He pressed play and pulled her down so that they were lying back on the grass, heads touching. She wanted to sit up to make sure nothing was going to sneak up on her, but she fought the urge and instead gripped Ronnie's hand tightly.

Melanie's voice seemed to bleed with loss and Caz too felt like weeping. She breathed and the music seemed to enter her lungs, slowing her heart, allowing the stars above to rush into her brain.

CHAPTER ELEVEN

Ronnie's chest rose and fell under Caz's palm. Afraid to wake him, she left her hand there and lifted her head up, straining her neck to check if they were alone. It was early, the sun nudging towards the horizon, spilling soft blue light out over the lawn and illuminating the quilted cloudscape above. Caz let her head fall back on the grass and listened to Ronnie breathe, the rhythm of her own breath matching his. His eyelids flickered and she hoped he wouldn't wake up. She'd say something stupid and a superior look would slide over his face. They were leaving that afternoon and she'd probably never see him again, best just to slip away taking this one perfect memory with her. She lifted her hand gently off his chest and he stirred and rolled away.

The sound of tiny birds trilling and chirruping splashed down from the treetops, clearing her head and buoying her up on the short journey back to the round house. Swinging her arms and taking in big breaths of fresh morning air, Caz felt alert and refreshed. The light was getting brighter, sharper and as she emerged into the clearing, she squinted slightly, surveying the devastated scene. The driveway was a minefield of shattered glass and discarded cans. Puke floated on the surface of the paddling pool attracting a thrumming black cloud of fat bluebottles and an anonymous casualty in an orange hoodie was asleep by the speakers, filthy trousers half pulled down to reveal a white bottom smeared with what Caz hoped was mud. Nobody else was about.

The door had been left open a crack, so Caz was able to sneak into the lounge without waking Suze and Ollie who were fast asleep on the sofa. Just looking around the room made her eyeballs hurt. The place had been trashed, childish felt tip pen doodles of spirals, fairies, curly piles of poop, stars, a cock and balls, spaceships and smiling flowers scrawled on the walls, floor littered with discarded branches.

Trying not to tread on anything, Caz picked her way across the room through to the kitchen, then made her way as quietly as she could up the stairs to the bedroom. Judging by the trail of muddy boot prints that lead from the door of the bedroom to the bathroom, and the fag butts floating in the toilet, she realized that people must have been coming through while Rosie slept. Caz opened a window to let out the smell of stale smoke that hung in the air. She knew from experience that it would cling to her clothes and the bedding and wondered if there'd be a chance to wash them before they left. In the bathroom, she filled a plastic cup with tap water and gulped it down. Something was off, it tasted metallic, tainted.

If anyone challenged her about being out all night, at least she could point out that it would have been impossible to get any sleep with drunken people trooping through on their way to the toilet. Reassuring herself that she had been wronged, Caz changed into her pyjamas, brushed her teeth and curled up in bed beside her comatose sister.

She was back in Upton Park, walking along freshly painted corridors, passing by rooms that glittered and sparkled. She herself was dressed in a beautiful blue dress that rustled as she glided up a staircase and floated into an elegant room. The blue Chinese vase had been filled with orchids and placed on top of a polished wooden table that stood beneath a glittering chandelier.

Free of dust, everything sparkled and gleamed brightly. She would have felt perfectly serene if it hadn't been for the sound of someone weeping nearby. Annoyed, she turned to her reflection in the mirror and was shocked to see that the contents of the room appeared to have been turned upside down and shaken around. This room was filthy, some of the bulbs in the chandelier were missing and junk was piled up everywhere. She too was different, wearing a grubby t-shirt and jeans, her hair a total mess. The weeping got louder and she realised that she was listening to Rosie, keening gently beside her in the bed. She kept her eyes shut and tried to return to her dream, but it was useless, she'd been ripped back into the real world.

As if sensing that Caz had now woken up, Rosie began to howl urgently. Pulsing through her brain in neon-bright jags, the noise was giving her a headache. The last time Rosie had cried like that was when she'd bit her lip open after falling down the stairs, red blood dripping from her mouth, staining the bright green fabric of her shirt black. Caz threw the covers off her head and sat up, the room rushing at her so fast it almost knocked her back down onto the mattress.

'What's wrong?' she asked angrily.

Rosie shook her head, huge tears plopping down her flushed cheeks. Outside van doors opened. With saliva pouring out of her nose and mouth, Rosie's purple face reminded Caz of a bruised split fruit, something you might grind underfoot if you found it lying on the filthy floor of a market.

The bedroom door opened and Tink rushed in. Without the tinkling of her jewellery to signal her approach, she could steal up on you without warning. Perhaps that's why she wore it, to anchor herself in reality. Without it she might just evaporate into thin air.

Tink perched next to Rosie at the edge of the bed.

'Love, what's the matter?' Tink said, softly, stroking Rosie's forehead. 'Did mummy's friends keep you up last night?'

Her sister dragged up a deep breath and through shuddering sobs that shook her frame, wailed, 'My legs hurt.'

Caz swung her legs round and sat with her head in her hands at the side of the bed. This wasn't about her. She'd got away with it.

Leaving Tink to deal with Rosie, Caz skulked off down the stairs and into the lounge. The sofa was empty so she sat down, legs pulled up against her chest, wondering if she might be able to get some more kip in.

'Oi oi! Morning! Where'd you disappear to last night, eh? Off with that posh lad, were we?' said Suze, strolling into the room.

Not waiting for Caz to reply, Suze went straight into the kitchen and began stuffing utensils and crockery into a canvas bag she'd brought with her.

'I was using that teapot,' said Caz, standing in the doorway.

'Easy come, easy go. To be fair, wasn't yours in the first place. Besides, it'll only take up space in your van. This way you can borrow it any time you want. Crying shame that all this stuff has gone to waste for so long when there's people out there who have nothing. '

Caz was sure that Suze was planning to flog most of the stuff she'd pilfered but knew better than to get into an argument over it. She wished she had the courage to pinch the pot back. At school they'd made an example of one girl for stealing a ruler, but at the squat and on the road it seemed other people's stuff was fair game, just as long as it wasn't nailed down.

'What's all the bother with Rosie upstairs?' asked Suze.

Caz shrugged, annoyed at the way Suze was casually making off with the contents of the kitchen after helping to trash the house.

'Be like that,' Suze stuck her tongue out.

Tink drifted down the stairs and hovered by the table, absentmindedly dipping her finger into a puddle of spilt beer and tracing out a wet flower on the plastic tablecloth.

'What's up with old Rosie then?' enquired Suze.

Tink looked at Suze, dazed. 'She says her legs hurt all of a sudden. I tried to move them, but she just started crying her eyes out. I've never seen her like this.' She sat down in a chair and sighed. 'Feeling a bit delicate myself as well. Could do without this drama.'

'Amen to that babe,' said Suze, pulling the cord shut on her bag.

'Do you think we should get a doctor Caz?' Tink said.

'You're asking me?' replied Caz, annoyed that her mum couldn't make a simple decision on her own.

'Better safe than sorry Tink,' put in Suze.

Tink stood for a moment, sucking the bottom of her lip, twirling her hair in her fingers, and staring out of the window, then turned and walked towards Chris' van, Caz trailing behind.

'Chris love, you up?' she said, banging on the door.

Chris stuck his head out, glassy eyes completely bloodshot, hair flattened on one side.

'Rosie's in a bad way, I need you to go up to the house to call for a doctor.'

'What right now? No cup of tea, no good morning kiss?'

Tink kissed his cheek and waited for him to get dressed.

Once Chris had set off for Upton Park, Caz pointed out that they'd have to at least attempt to tidy the house, seeing as the doctor might be turning up any minute. They roused the others and set them, groaning, to help clear things up a bit. Itching to go off to Tipton, they dragged their feet and milled around, half-heartedly picking up the odd can and dumping them in carrier bags. Without anything bigger to store the rubbish in, in the end they resorted to dragging the pool over to the woods, tipping out the stagnant water and puke onto the ground, then filling the thing with empties, before folding it over and hiding it behind a bush. The branches also got chucked away, but, after scrubbing at the carpet and the walls for a bit, they decided that there wasn't much they could do to clean up the muddy boot prints and felt tip 'art.' Lacy had been at the party himself, so he could hardly complain. At least the bloke in the grubby orange top had removed himself and his nasty looking bum from the driveway.

Even though it was her idea, Caz deeply resented having to help with the clean-up operation but didn't complain too much in case someone brought up the fact that she hadn't been at the party. They had probably all been way too wasted to notice anyway. The relief she felt at not being caught turned into resentment when Caz realized that Tink didn't really seem to care about where she'd been.

While Caz scrubbed the plates at the sink, Rosie was sitting upstairs being treated like a princess. She'd been given the radio from the kitchen and was listening to the charts while dipping her fingers into a jar of chocolate spread. Caz slammed the crockery down hard on the draining board, vaguely hoping that something would shatter and she'd cut herself. Tink, taking a break from mooning ineffectually round the house, sat down the kitchen table. Oblivious to Caz's rage, she stared out of the window with a sorrowful look on her face. Chris, back from Upton Park, was putting his feet up and smoking a fag. Ollie rapped on the doorframe to get their attention.

'Everything alright, Tink?' he asked. 'Just me and Suze have been thinking it might be time to head off in the van.'

'No worries, it's all fine. We're going to wait for the doc, says he's going to swing by in a couple of hours, then we'll be right behind you,' said Chris, optimistically.

'Well, we might end up going down tomorrow. Depending on what the doctor says, I don't see us moving Rosie today, do you Caz?' said Tink.

Caz kept her back to them and shrugged her shoulders.

'Think you can handle things without me for a bit?' Chris asked Ollie.

'Sure, safe. But you'll be down tomorrow, right? Won't be much of a party without speakers, or indeed, your good selves.' Ollie replied.

'No yeah, definitely. We're just worried about old Rosalie you know. Anyway, you lot best make tracks now if you want to be there before dark.'

'Alright captain. I'll let the others know and we'll make a move.'

Once they'd all gone, Caz sneaked off to have a snooze on the sofa. The rain started up while she was asleep and when Doctor Green arrived in the late afternoon, she awoke to his strong scent of wet wool, antiseptic, sweat and tobacco smoke.

'Is this her?' He pointed at Caz, who'd just been startled from a deep sleep.

'No, that's the oldest, Rosie's upstairs,' said Tink, apologetically.

'Is there something wrong with you too, eh? No reason to be lazing around on the sofa in the middle of the day,' he shouted at her.

He took in the felt tip pen drawings and boot marks on the floor and gave her a horsey snort of disdain, then followed Tink up the stairs, noisily bumping his leather bag into the walls. Caz wrapped herself in her mother's shawl and walked over to the window, placing her forehead against the cold glass. A shoal of silver raindrops collided with the windowpane. Upstairs Rosie began to howl and the trees swayed overhead as if their creaking limbs were also wracked in pain. Another movement, closer to the ground, at odds with this slow swaying, a flailing, like that of a dying fish, caught Caz's eye. Something large and white was struggling wildly in the branches. As she watched the thing twist in the wind her throat tightened. But then she realized; it was only a plastic bag caught in the tree.

'Perhaps it's all in her head.'

Startled, Caz swung round to discover that the doctor had re-entered the room. Shoulders slumped and heavy head hanging forward, as if bearing more than his fair share of human misery, he collapsed into the sofa and scanned the room with glassy green eyes. The slack flesh on his face seemed to be melting around his red rimmed eyeballs and when his aggrieved gaze swivelled in Caz's direction, she turned away, sickened.

'But we can't rule out the possibility that the underlying cause is something more serious. Just to be sure, we should book her in to see a specialist,' Doctor Green paused and looked at the horrible drawings on the wall. 'I understand you're not local.'

'Just passing through,' Chris replied.

Caz was having trouble breathing. The air seemed to have thinned. She looked at her hands and feet; they appeared to be 100 miles away and her head felt like it had ballooned up to twice its normal size. Every time she looked up, someone was looking at her.

'That makes things rather difficult. Normally I'd refer her right away. Where are you based?'

She had to escape, but when she shifted in her chair the doctor's eyes slid back in her direction, rooting her to the spot. She needed to pee badly.

'Up in Kentish Town, London, but we weren't planning on going back till September. Do you think we should go back now? Is it serious?' Tink said, her voice going posh for the doctor.

'It's really not my field, as I said, it could be psychological. Has Rosie had any recent trauma perhaps? Has she witnessed anything upsetting?'

'Could just be growing pains though innit doc,' said Chris.

'Growing pains generally occur at night and affect the limbs only when sedentary. The symptoms simply don't fit. As I said, it's best to have it checked out as soon as possible, but I don't see the harm in waiting a week. It would be difficult to move her in her current condition in any case. My advice is to keep her still with as little stimulus as possible, a bored child will quickly snap out of play acting. Especially if they're not getting the attention they need, so it's important not to pander to her.' Doctor Green stood up to leave. 'I'm sorry I couldn't shed more light on this problem, but as I said, it's a matter for an expert.'

Once the doctor was out the door, Caz raced to the toilet to pee. The rain outside pattered on the windowpane and she sat for a while, knickers round her ankles, enjoying the temporary privacy of the toilet. Mind a blank, she gazed at a patch of damp plaster in the corner of the room.

'We can't just up and leave, not with Rosie in this state.'

Though Tink's voice penetrated through the door, she couldn't quite make out what Chris was saying. As she strained to listen, scrunched up faces began to worm their way into the bumps and lumps in the plaster, faces like the ones she'd seen in the trees the night before, twisted in pain, howling silently, trapped in the walls.

Chris' voice began again to rumble incoherently at a pitch too low to penetrate through the wood.

'They'll be other parties. You don't seriously think you're the only DJ out there. You want to get your priorities straight.'

The muffled bass began to thrum again in her ears.

'If you think you're so important to other people, why don't you just fuck off and go then.'

Caz heard a door slam. When she finally got the courage to leave the loo, she found Chris sat on the sofa. He looked sheepishly up at her and smiled weakly.

'Your mum's just popped out for a bit. We'll probably be off to Tipton tomorrow morning instead of today, seeing as Rosie's a bit off colour. Fancy a bite of toast or something?'

CHAPTER TWELVE

Chris was in the doghouse. Even after sloping off to ask for permission from Lacy to stay another night, he hadn't been forgiven. Instead, Tink ignored him and cuddled up with Rosie, reading her fairy stories all evening and even falling asleep in her bed, leaving Chris to sleep on his own in the van. Caz, of course, would be sleeping on the sofa.

The next day it seemed that Rosie too had cooled towards Chris. Gripping the bedsheet to her chest when he entered the room, she refused to respond to any of the bribes he offered in exchange for setting off for Tipton and wept at even the suggestion of moving downstairs.

They had all been gathered round Rosie's bed, trying to decide what to do when Chris frowned and asked Tink if they couldn't 'have a quick word' downstairs. After they'd gone, Caz went over to the window. In the distance, the manor sat squat and sombre above a boiling tumult of foliage. A volley of raindrops battered the windowpane.

'You know we can't stay, don't you? I mean we're pushing our luck as it is,' said Caz.

Rosie didn't reply.

'You know what I think. I think you're faking it, like that time you didn't want to go to school and drank a bottle of Tabasco to make yourself puke.'

At first it seemed like Rosie hadn't heard her. The rain continued to fall steadily outside. It wouldn't be much fun setting up camp in Tipton with the weather like this.

'Mr Lacy wants us to stay. He needs us to find his little girl,' she said quietly but firmly, as if stating some indisputable fact.

'You are completely off your nut. You do know that, don't you?'

Though they were looking each other in the eye, Rosie didn't seem to be focussing on Caz, it was as if she was looking beyond humdrum reality into some other private world. That was the aggravating thing about Rosie, there was no appealing to her sense of logic because she inhabited a totally different universe. Reasoning with her was like trying to explain the rules of Scrabble to a cat.

Outside, the noise of Chris' engine gunning in the driveway seemed to blast a hole in her chest. Gravel churned beneath the tires, mangling her insides. They weren't going to Tipton after all, they were stranded again. Maybe now she could get Tink to call grandma and granddad and they could finally go back to Radlett.

She found Tink crumpled up on the sofa in the lounge. This latest tragedy seemed to have shrunk her mother even more, so that her flesh barely filled the folds of loose fabric.

'Mum?'

Tink didn't respond but continued to nibble at the sides of her nails, tearing off tiny strips of skin. Not even wincing when a bauble of blood formed on one of the raw slivers of exposed flesh, but instead gazing at it with an abstracted look of satisfaction.

'Mum.' She took Tink's hand away from her mouth. 'Shall I call grandma and granddad to come and get us?'

Tink looked at Caz. Unable to keep it together any longer, her eyes filled with tears. She put her head on Caz's shoulder. Automatically, Caz raised a stiff arm and patted the ridges of bone on her mother's spine.

'Rosie hasn't eaten breakfast, I'm going to get her a bowl of cereal,' she said. There wouldn't be any reasoning with her mum when she was in this kind of state, best mention getting back to

Radlett later.

Tink drew back and tried to reign in her sobs, making a snotty choking sound as she did so that made Caz want to gag. Her mother was revoltingly weak. Caz wondered why she couldn't cry in the bathroom like a normal person. She'd once overheard Suze say that for a tiny person, Tink had a massive amount of emotional baggage. It was true; it was as if Tink kept dropping her heavy suitcases, spilling the messy contents all over the floor and expecting Caz to help pick things up.

Caz went into the kitchen and took a shaky breath. She ought to make breakfast. Granddad was always saying that as long as you had a good breakfast inside you, you could face the day. She found a pan and went to the sink to fill it up. Turning the tap too fast, water splashed up off the metal surface, drenching the front of her t-shirt. When she tried to dry it off with a tea towel, she realised too late that the towel had been used to wipe up the mud off the floor.

The streak of dirt on her one remaining clean t-shirt confirmed Caz's premonition that the day was already spoiled. She would just have to put her head down to ride it out. When she'd been little, her dad used to stroke her hair after a day like this and sing her a sad song about an old horse, the idea being that there was always someone worse off than you. But her dad wasn't there, and Chris had left without saying goodbye. She picked up the pan and threw it on the floor, surprising herself with the force of her anger. She kicked the pan again for good measure, stubbing her toe in the process, then threw the tea towel to the floor. She looked around for something better, something that would smash, but as she did so, the anger drained out of her, and her eyes filled up.

Sitting at the table, she drew in a deep shaky breath and held back the tears. She wasn't like Tink. She didn't have to weigh other people down with her problems. The effort of keeping down the tears was swelling and hardening her throat. She needed tea, but the thought that Suze had taken her teapot jabbed at her, and instead of throwing something else, she grabbed a handful of hair and pulled hard. 'Breathe,' she thought, remembering the exercises the doctor had taught her. Eventually she managed to switch the kettle on, wash out a mug, and find a teabag and a tiny amount of milk. There wasn't enough milk for Tink, but who cared?

Once Caz had drunk her tea, she got round to making Rosie some breakfast. She wasn't up to making an egg. There was too much that could go wrong today. She might end up setting the house on fire or wind up in the hospital with third-degree burns. Rosie would have to have Weetabix with water, but at least there were a few sachets of sugar left from the stash Caz had pilfered from the service station.

Rosie didn't complain that there wasn't any milk in her Weetabix. To Caz, watching her sister dutifully munch down her brown, sugar-covered slop, this was as good as a confession that the pains in her legs were fake. She had made a bowl for herself too but gave up after trying to force a few mouthfuls down her constricted throat. Rosie continued to dolefully munch her breakfast and the noise of food sloshing around in her mouth filled the room, until Caz felt like smashing her sister in the gob.

Trying to get herself under control, she picked up her book and began to read. As her eyes ran along the lines of text, her thoughts took a different track: perhaps she ought to see if Tink was alright? She could go down to the village and call grandma and granddad. She had the number in her pocket after all. But she'd never been to the village and didn't know which direction to start out in or even how far it was. Could she ask Ronnie for help? She didn't want him to know they were stranded. He might alert Lacy to the problem. They didn't need any help. If they could just get back to London...

She turned the page and realised that she hadn't followed the story at all. The doorbell rang, an ugly rusted buzz that Caz could feel in her teeth. A muffled male voice could be heard downstairs.

'It's Roopert,' whispered Rosie.

Caz realised that she couldn't stay out of the conversation

again. Chris had left and no one had consulted her. Not that she cared, but she couldn't trust her mum to make any decisions now. She pushed herself off the bed and made her way back to the lounge.

Lacy's hand sat motionless, covering Tink's knee, the large blue veins above his fingers twitching below his pallid skin.

'Catherine, how are we today, hmm?' he said, showing her his teeth. There was something red stuck between them. Perhaps he'd stopped off to consume some tiny forest creature on the way there and hadn't had time to pick them clean.

'Your mother and I have just been having a chat and we've decided it's best for Rosie if you all move up to the house, at least until she's up on her feet again. I really can't have you staying here anymore,' he said, looking around pointedly at the horrible scrawling on the walls and the dirt on the floor.

Caz flushed red, ashamed of how they lived, of how the others had trashed the neat little house, of how weak her mother was. She'd come down too late. If only she'd given her mum a proper hug, they might be walking to the village now to call grandma and granddad. Caz tried to look Lacy in the eye, to show him he didn't intimidate her, but her gaze immediately fled to the faded flower-patterned curtains. His eyes were as blue as the veins on his hands and when she looked at them, she felt odd. It was an unpleasant sensation, like biting into potato instead of ice cream. Something unexpected that turned her stomach.

'I thought we could go to stay with grandma and granddad, mum,' she said, looking at the floor, head bent.

'We can't get the trailer back without Chris' van, and you know granddad can't drive long distances with his hip. Besides, Chris has promised he'll be back at the end of the weekend,' Tink said, as if all this were perfectly reasonable.

She wanted to tell Tink about the missing girl, about the room full of swords, but couldn't bring herself to mention it in front of Lacy. Besides, what did she really know about it? He might get angry if she mentioned it and she should be careful to stay on his good side. She stared at the sun-bleached flowers, defeated. Except for those intense eyes and pulsing veins, every-thing in the room seemed drained of colour.

'But you just said...'

'I just said Chris won't be back for a while, he hasn't gone for good. He's got other responsibilities you know. He's not your dad, we can't expect him to drop everything. Of course, I'm not 100 percent with that, but it's like people have their own karma to deal with and we're just part of the equation...'

As Tink twittered, she avoided Caz's eye and instead con-centrated on twirling a strand of hair in her fingers. She picked up a lighter and began burning off the split ends that spiked off the tight bronze coil. The acrid scent of burned hair reminded Caz of the time her dad had left. Lacy reached out and held her hands still, preventing her from setting fire to anything else. She looked at him, flushed.

'Sorry, weird. I mean it's weird. Bad habit, sorry.'

'You don't need to apologise to me. You have done nothing to be ashamed of,' he said in a hypnotist's monotone, all the while continuing to restrain her.

Caz's stomach churned as she watched her mother blush and squirm in his grip.

Finally, he released her. 'That's settled then. Do you want to start getting your things together?'

Up in the bedroom Tink edged cautiously towards the bed, 'Hello Rosie love, we'll be staying with Mr Lacy for a while. But that means we're going to have to move you, so you'll have to be brave for just a little bit.'

Rosie nodded and then turned to Lacy, holding her arms out to him. When he lifted her off the bed, she whimpered slightly, clutching Lacy tightly with her small fingers and bury-ing her head in his neck. His eyes were glistening triumphantly as he straightened up and carefully made his way down the stairs.

Abandoning the trailer outside the round house, they walked through the woods to Lacy's car. A rucksack hastily stuffed full of dirty laundry was slung into the boot. The invalid sat up front, and Caz and Tink in the back. Under a blank grey sky, the car glided along the curved driveway and eased to a halt in front of the entrance to Upton Park. They got out and walked up the stairs. Rain was falling in a fine mist, beading their hair and clothes with tiny droplets of silver. But the jewelled effect lasted no longer than a minute and, as the water seeped into cloth, Caz's clothes stuck to her skin leaving her shivering and cold in the dark hallway.

PART THREE

CHAPTER THIRTEEN

What Lacy called 'supper' had been a cold congealed mess of stringy meat and disintegrating potatoes, served up in such an imposing setting that Caz felt she had to eat the whole thing. If Chris had been there, Caz could have fed half of it to Sid, but failing that, she asked for a bottle of ketchup, her words rebounding off the vaulted ceiling, amplifying the nervous wobble in her voice, so the echo impacted like a smack in the face, silencing her for the rest of the meal. The gaudy plastic bottle that was eventually brought to the table seemed to offend the grand ladies whose portraits hung on the wall opposite her – the pair regarding the vulgar object with silent disdain.

'It's been an age since I ate in here. Rather dusty and gloomy I'm afraid.' Lacy sat at the head of the table, his voice booming confidently around the room. 'I don't think I've eaten here since I got back from Japan. One worries that it's too much trouble for Mrs Dixon.'

Mrs Dixon didn't seem to have troubled herself too much, neither with the meal, nor with laying the table, only half of which had been cleared for dinner. The other half remained loaded with antique junk. An off-white tablecloth covered in wax and greasy stains had been thrown over the end they sat at. More wax dripped from a large brass candelabra in the centre of the table that gave out nearly as much light as the dim chandelier above. Having slathered her food in ketchup, Caz now struggled with the heavy silver cutlery and a cut crystal goblet. Cosily tucked up in bed at the top of the house, Rosie had escaped this ordeal.

Tink, subdued by the heavy atmosphere and the recent departure of Chris, hadn't said much, but finally roused herself to ask, 'Why did you go to Japan then?'

'I went to study Zen Buddhism. Don't get me wrong, I'm not a religious nut or anything. But perhaps you'll understand. Caz tells me you meditate too,' said Lacy.

Tink nodded her head like crazy, her dangly earrings jangling. She took a gulp of wine and looked uncertainly about her. 'Totally well, right, you know I find, right, that religion is just such a lot of crap, of course I mean look at all the wars it's caused and all those gaudy cathedrals and that, it's just about money, but I do believe that we are all spiritual and that like if we can tap into that, we can feed into that energy that runs through all of us. I'm not into God as some bloke with a beard in the sky. I reckon God is in us all, we're all spiritual...' Tink trailed off.

'Hmm.' Lacy frowned at her. An awful pause opened up a yawning chasm between them. He cleared his throat. 'It sounds like you have a lot more faith than I in the benevolence of the universe. To accept spirituality, one has to accept the idea of some kind of guiding force, some intelligent plan, and that is something that just doesn't tally with my experience of life.'

'So you're not like into karma or anything?' asked Tink.

'Mum, he just said he doesn't believe in any of that hippie rubbish,' said Caz.

'No, on the contrary, karma is a concept that came out of Buddhism, but I feel that it's somehow been subverted into a kind of cosmic cash register, when really it's all about helping out your fellow man.'

'Like you just helped us out.' Tink raised her glass to him. 'But what I don't get is that if you're into Buddhism, why not go to India? I mean that's where it all got started right? My friend right, she went to Nepal.'

'Nepal isn't in India mum,' Caz interjected.

Tink pretended not to notice. 'She came back, like, transformed. She was always someone who gave off a great vibe, but now you can practically feel her aura. You feel good after seeing her, you know what I mean. It's like we're all so imprisoned by our own negative energy that we block out the good stuff that naturally runs through us all, I've always thought that there's some energy in the universe that we can connect to, that runs through us all. Tap into that universality and you're like liberated.'

As she spoke, Lacy looked down at his hands and held down the rotating thumb with his index finger, smiling ever so slightly. When she'd done babbling, he looked down the far end of the table towards the mess of random objects.

'For me, it was a little different. More than getting in touch with a higher power, Zen promised me some level of control over my own mind at a time when I felt that I was ready to implode. Zen is Buddhism stripped of mysticism, pomp and ceremony, more a philosophy than a religion. There's something inherently weak in turning to a deity, an imagined patriarchal figure to give us comfort when life has knocked us around. One must learn to stand on one's own two feet, because when it comes down to it, we're all terribly alone. Relying on a higher being as a kind of mental crutch is just setting yourself up for a fall. Besides, I don't want to be reincarnated, god forbid that one should have to live out more than one lifetime.

'And why Japan, well, I'd always been interested in samurai warriors, I have a collection of swords, a rather gruesome interest I suppose. The samurai had a rigid code of conduct, incredible mental discipline and this was partly down to their study of Zen, it allowed them to live in the moment and in doing so, conquer their fear of death, their fear of killing. But it's more than a tool for warriors, through Zazen, the practise of meditation, the mind is calmed. Meditation liberates one's mind from fear, fear of pain, anxiety, all the torments that plague us. It gives us equilibrium.

'Perhaps Zen developed in Japan because the Japanese are

a rather dispassionate race who have learned to control themselves in the face of terrible tragedies. You have to understand that Japan is a country of extremes. The climate ranges from freezing cold in winter to unbearably hot and humid in summer. It's racked by earthquakes and the occasional tsunami, devastating whole regions every few decades or so. That means the people have developed a kind of stoicism. They have a strength that I admire. Resilient, self-reliant and most importantly, not in the least bit interested in me, beyond a cursory polite curiosity.

'I could and did go days without speaking to anybody. Japanese culture seemed to be, ah, seemed to be coated in shiny black lacquer. It's smooth, attractive, but your fingers just slip off it when you try to really grasp its core meaning. But that's what I wanted, a mystery. I was sickened by people in England, it was as if I could see through them, see their organs, their nasty small-minded thoughts. I didn't want to know what was in people's heart of hearts, I wanted to be somewhere where I couldn't penetrate the surface of things. That was Japan. Everybody was kind, courteous and polite, but nobody told me what they were really thinking. It's like stepping into another reality, a parallel universe.

'After spending some time there as a tourist, I began my studies into Zen by taking a week's retreat in Kamakura, a peaceful town on the coast close to Tokyo. It was run by a monk who spoke English and, of course, attended by a bunch of foreigners. Luckily, most of our time was spent in silence, meditating in a beautiful room high up on the hillside, sliding doors open to the elements. It was late summer, and the weather was terribly humid, making one drowsy even with the fresh mountain breeze.

'My Zen master was a kind old man with a mischievous sense of humour and my fellow classmates a bunch of amiable, if slightly woolly-minded, travellers who were there for a quick digestible gobbet of Japanese Buddhism, something to tell the folks back home about. They found themselves rather put out with the lengthy amounts of time they were expected to sit and meditate. I hated it for a different reason. For me the meditation didn't last long enough. I wanted to sit for hours on end with pins and needles prickling my legs. I craved a cold snap that would refresh my heat-drugged mind. I shunned the others and read some literature on Zen, much of it badly translated, so that I began to develop the idea that to really overcome mental suffering, one must also learn to tolerate and rise above physical pain.

'I woke earlier and earlier in the day, only took cold showers, ate little, and yet still I hadn't satisfied my desire to mortify the flesh. I believed I was learning to rise above the eternal cycle of pain and suffering that is our lot in life, but in actual fact was plunging myself deeper into the stuff. It was as if I'd decided that misery was my lot. In a twisted way I enjoyed it, I felt I deserved it. But what I was actually doing was using pain to block out spiritual suffering. Not very enlightened I'm afraid.

'I became impatient with my master, who I felt had been corrupted by western notions during his time at a Buddhist monastery in England. He allowed the students to use cushions when they sat for long periods meditating, a practise I disdained. I suppose I was being petty, but I felt that it took the whole point of the exercise away. I left and went to Kyoto, visiting Zazen temples in the area and hardly speaking to a soul.

'There I heard about a pilgrimage called the Kumano Kodo. The pilgrimage is actually a number of different sacred routes through the remote Kii Mountains, paths that a retired emperor had trodden back in ancient times. It was just the thing I'd been looking for: a punishing walk between ancient shrines through jagged mountain scenery. If I chose the right route, it could take weeks to complete. This was landscape carpeted in dense forest that had been violently formed through centuries of volcanic activity. Sometimes up mountains so high that you're right up in the clouds. And that's where it gets dangerous, because people have wandered off the path in these conditions and died of exposure. I chose the toughest route, of course, and, not able to tolerate travel companions, I travelled alone.

'To communicate, I had a basic knowledge of Japanese that

I'd acquired during my time there. It was enough to ask for a glass of water, or to find out whether I could stay the night at a temple or inn.

'The first few days went by without incident. I walked along the paths, going higher and higher up. Each day the track becoming lonelier and lonelier. Other hikers would greet me with a curt *konichiwa* and nod as they passed but would never try to engage me further in conversation. To my delight, I saw no other foreigners, so I managed to avoid the cloying intimacy that one's compatriots force upon you while abroad.

'Autumn had begun, and the air was bracing, fresh. Each day I'd push myself to walk just a little bit further, so that by the time I was forced to stop at dusk I would eat the briefest of meals, take a bath and then collapse into bed, exhausted. I was finally sleeping soundly, unaware of any nasty dreams I might have been having.

'In the second week, I caught a cold. It dulled my senses, made my head feel woolly and this too I enjoyed, as if a thin tissue-like substance was separating me from the rest of the world. My limbs ached and I needed to rest up for a day or so, to recover, but I liked that pain, it felt right. By the time I stumbled upon a rather run-down looking shrine just as the sun was setting, I was feeling extremely queer.

'The place was the stuff of Japanese ghost stories, with numerous yellowing seals stuck onto the peeling red paint of its main gate. The gate itself guarded by moss-covered stone foxes, their lips curled back in a threatening snarl – warning me to stay away. The rustling of fallen autumn leaves seemed to signal the arrival of mountain spirits.

'I crept round the side of the main shrine building to a nondescript wooden structure at the back. Nobody appeared for a long time, and I was just about to leave when a young monk arrived at the door. He looked a little taken aback at the sight of a foreigner, and I foolishly thought that having lived all his life in this isolated spot, it might perhaps have been the first time he'd ever seen a *gaijin*. I greeted him again in my faltering

Japanese, *Konichiwa, tabi o shiteimasu. Ippaku tomarimasuka.* The monk peered at me and then replied in near perfect American-accented English. "Of course you can stay the night. It would be my pleasure. It's been ages since I've had the chance to practise my English."

'I was furious: here I was on the other side of the world, finally in a place so isolated that I had only seen one other person on my journey that day and I bump into a Japanese monk not only fluent in English, but hungry for conversation and news of the outside world. He took me back into his private room and sat me down in an easy chair, the first time I'd sat in a Western chair in over a week, and poured me a glass of Scotch. The room was filled with jazz records and in the corner was a trumpet.

'I discovered that Keisuke was a reluctant monk. He'd been born to it, so when his father passed away, he had been summoned back from New York to the shrine to fulfil his duties. Before that he'd been happily bumming around, working as a waiter by day and playing jazz by night. A fascinating chap really, and I regret the way I behaved with him, sullen and withdrawn.

'In his excitement to talk, Keisuke had forgotten to feed me and what with my cold, the whisky and lack of food, I began to nod off. He kept on talking and talking and at some moment I passed out. I woke with a blanket over me and a futon made out on the floor in front of me. But, starving hungry with a raging headache, I slept fitfully after that. I spent most of the night concentrating on my breathing exercises and trying to convince myself that it was a minor discomfort that could easily be surmounted with some mental discipline.

'The next morning, I woke late and found Keisuke sweeping the grounds of the temple, it was hard to believe that the heart of a jazz musician beat within this simply-dressed monk. Quickly nodding to him, I hurried past and entered the shrine, then sat meditating. It is better to meditate on an empty stomach in the morning, but if you haven't had anything to eat the night before, it really makes a nonsense of the act. Starving, my head began to swim as I sat down and closed my eyes. Cartoon images of Bugs Bunny began swirling in my head along with a refrain from one of the records Keisuke had played me the night before, I think it might have been *A Love Supreme*, you know, Coltrane. Anyway, I couldn't simply dismiss them and put them to one side. The same inane repetitive images and motifs kept coming back to me, like a swarm of insects that are impossible to swat away.

'Rather than putting this down to my hunger, the cold and the high altitude, I blamed Keisuke. He had polluted my pure state of isolation. I had to leave there as soon as possible to avoid being further infected by his enthusiasm for the superficial trappings of Western culture. Grabbing my bag from the hallway, I brusquely told him that I was heading off to the village that lay a half day's walk from that spot. He looked disappointed and puzzled but allowed me to leave.

'My stomach was by then making the strangest of noises, but I didn't listen. It's one thing to teach oneself to ignore every minor physical irritation, quite another to completely ignore one's basic physical needs. As I climbed the steep path, my heart was pounding in my chest and my head was throbbing.

'I hurried up the slope, past a group of red bonneted *jizo* statues that stood by the side of the road. Weather worn, the features of the stone monks were now disturbingly blank. I'd never been fond of these statues because they had a disconcerting connection to the source of my own misery. It's said that Jizo protects infants and children in the afterlife and bereaved mothers place red bonnets and bibs on his statue in thanks. For me the figures have a funereal aspect and although Jizo is also said to guide travellers safely, I would always hurry past these creepy figures.

'At first, I didn't notice it, because my eyes had already been fogging up. You know how it is when you get sick or too hungry and a kind of fine mist seems to descend over everything? So I kept going forward up and up the mountain and further and further into the fog. I had only been going about an hour and a half and there were still at least a couple more hours of my journey left, but I couldn't even make out the path ahead. I sat down to catch my breath and that's when I heard the bells.

'It had to be another hiker, coming down the path in the opposite direction. If I followed the sound, then I could continue my journey. But noises are hard to pinpoint out on a mountain-top, the wind can whip them around so they seem to be coming from a different direction, and that's how I lost my way on the path. I began going down the hill, lost my footing and skidded until I fell hard against a huge tree. Completely disorientated, I heard a strange ticking sound and it took me awhile to realise that it was the noise of my own teeth chattering. It was early autumn, and though it was warm in the sunlight, in the shade it could be very cold, especially when the fog descended.

'I kicked the tree in irritation and shrugged off my rucksack to search inside for a warm top, balancing it on a rock. But my hand slipped, sending the blasted thing bouncing down the hillside into the thick murk. So there I was, stuck without any warmth, sick as a dog, starving hungry, my wallet and passport gone down the mountain, irretrievable. But still I wanted to forge forward. I just had to get away from Keisuke. Utterly absurd, I know.'

The door opened and Mrs Dixon walked in. She surveyed the remains of Caz's meal with a look of disapproval, then began to noisily collect the plates. Caz would have liked to offer to help her, but she didn't want to miss out on the end of the story.

'Mind if I smoke?' Tink said, taking out her baccy tin.

'Not at all, I might indulge in a puff too if you don't mind.'

'I can make you one, it's no trouble.'

'No, a little bit of yours will be fine.'

Tink lit up, took a few puffs and passed her cigarette to Lacy. He inhaled deeply and sat watching the blue smoke curl and unfurl upwards.

'The fog was so thick that when I saw a shrouded dark shape just off to one side, I realized that the person must have been very close, so close I could almost touch them. Again, I heard the jingle of bells. Pilgrims on the route traditionally use staffs that have bells on the top, so this wasn't anything uncommon. It's so other travellers can hear them and be guided safely back to the path. I struck out in the direction of the traveller and, after taking a couple of steps, fell straight down a steep drop.

'I must have conked right out for a second because I don't remember the fall. When I woke, all the air had gone right out of me and I could hear a ringing in my ears. My left leg had crumpled under me and when I tried to stand, I felt the most excruciating pain. I'm ashamed to say I howled out loud. A horrible, lonely sound out there in the middle of nowhere. I must have sounded like some terrible animal. The traveller I'd seen made no reply.

'I don't know how long I was there, shivering, clinging onto a tree for dear life, shouting for help every now and again, teeth chattering like castanets playing a death rattle. But I knew that the only way to go was up, to try to find the path again. Somehow it was hard to get the gumption up to move at all. If I just relaxed into it, it wasn't so bad down there. I even began to feel a nice warm glow.

'From somewhere very far away I heard Keisuke saying, "Wake up you stupid fucking English man." But I believed that that had been a hallucination, because finally when I came to, the mist had cleared and there was not a soul around. I was lying on a narrow ledge with a steep drop below me, I'd fallen about ten feet down a sharp slope and with my leg in the state it was I had no idea how I would get back up.

'Unless someone came by before dark, I'd likely die of exposure during the night. I waited a long time there until finally something amazing happened; a rope dropped down just beside my head. It was Keisuke. Realising that it was too dangerous to climb down, he'd gone back for rope. He'd made a noose and told me to wrap it round my waist, then began to haul me up. It took a long time to get me up as I had barely any strength left. Keisuke pulled and I feebly tried to help. Finally, after a huge effort, I reached the path again and lay there for a while, shaking, covered in mud, while Keisuke caught his breath. How he had it in him to get me back to the shrine in that state, I don't know.

'He took me in and nursed me back to health. I had a twisted ankle and a nasty cold that took more than two weeks to cure. During that time, I learnt something from Keisuke that eventually led me to come back here, back home. In addition to his love of jazz, he had a deep sense of duty to the place he had been born a guardian of. He was proud of the shrine and enjoyed showing guests round, sharing its history with them. He might not have been the religious master I was looking for, but he reminded me that I had a place I was tied to too. I had a tradition to maintain. I had to come home here. Like me, Keisuke was alone, his mother having passed on a year after his father, but he didn't grumble once.

'Without my passport and any money, it wasn't easy to get home, but with some cash Keisuke had lent me, I finally made it to the British embassy in Tokyo. They helped me make my way back. I insisted on getting his address so I could forward him some funds, but he told me that the best thing I could do would be to promise that if I ever came across anyone in need, I would pay his kindness on to them. This was his sense of karma. The way I see it, you all dropped in here to help me pay that back to Keisuke.'

'Who was the traveller?' Caz asked, forgetting her shyness. 'Was it a ghost?'

'Keisuke and I differed on this point. He claims he didn't see anyone coming down the path in the opposite direction, but he wasn't too worried about it. Like many Japanese he is deeply superstitious and he told me that he believed the traveller could have been Jizo trying to guide me home. But if it was a spirit, I don't think its intentions were friendly. It was trying to lead me off a cliff after all.'

CHAPTER FOURTEEN

It had been a bad night. Bound to the bed in tight starched white sheets, the ancient house creaking beneath her, Caz strained to listen for other signs of life, for movement in the room next door where Rosie lay, apparently still paralysed. But the only creature making any noise had been a solitary owl hooting from inside the wood, the noise rippling out, then sinking without trace into the inky night. Her imagination conjured up squirming images of strange pale things worming their way out under cover of darkness. It wasn't until light began seeping through the curtains and the birds began to cheerfully babble to each other that she was finally able to get to some proper sleep.

Now she'd woken late and had no idea what time it was. When she'd got up about an hour ago, she had found her breakfast out by the door: a glass of orange juice, two cold slices of buttered toast and marmalade, a couple of Dairylea cheese triangles, and a cup of tea gone cold in the mug.

She lay back under the bright white quilt, gripping her Walkman tightly. The Bruce Springsteen album she was listening to reminded her of being on the Harley, wrapping her arms tightly around her dad's waist, with the cold air stinging her face as they sped down country lanes. She'd lean into corners just like he told her to, the engine revving as he turned the handlebars, sparks of sunlight leaping through the tangled foliage above. They'd stop off at some country pub, sharing a bag of crisps on a wooden picnic table. Leather and motor oil mixed with salt and vinegar flavour on her fingers as she licked them clean. Her dad would always get crisps in his beard and foam from his pint around his mouth.

What hurt most was that she could never get past the image of his ginger beard, never recall what his face looked like, only that he had green eyes and hair curling out of his ears. That morning, those fragments of memory were so sharp that they almost stung, bringing tears to her eyes.

A spear of sunlight struck the wooden boards at the foot of the bed, illuminating gilded specks of dust that buzzed, giving off flashes of pink and green as they drifted slowly to the floor; the fabric of reality disrupted as if the scene were about to morph in front of her sleep deprived eyes. The music too began to warp, sinking rapidly into a sonic sludge before grinding to a halt.

It had happened before, but this time she hadn't pressed stop in time. When she took the cassette out, the machine had had plenty of time to mangle the tape, making it impossible to extract it whole. The tiny metal cogs chewing up the last trace of her dad. She pulled the ribbon of gunmetal grey plastic gently, but it refused to budge, then yanked it hard till the tape dug into the flesh of her fingers.

A shout rang out in the garden. Caz got out of bed to investigate. From her window she had a bird's eye view of Tink running barefoot across the lawn below, laughing as she sank her toes into soft grass. Lacy, stooped, tray in hand, followed behind. Her window was slightly open bringing in the drowsy succulent smell of expensive blossoms. A table had been set out for lunch on the lawn, white cloth, sparkling glass, cut flowers. Lacy pulled a chair out for Tink and waited until she'd sat down to take his own seat. Bending over her he muttered something in her ear making Tink squirm in her seat and giggle, twisting her curly blonde hair coquettishly between her fingers. When they'd first met him, he'd made Tink twist and squirm in shame, now she was wriggling with delight. Disgusted, Caz stormed out of her room and charged into Rosie's room next door without knocking.

Dressed up in a smart navy shirt with a bright white Peter Pan collar, Rosie was sat up in bed, propped against some pillows. Brushed hair gleaming in the sunlight, she was sitting unnaturally still, hands loosely clasped in her lap with a faraway look in her eyes, like someone had arranged her into a pose so she could have her portrait painted. The old record player had been moved into her room and was playing classical music loudly.

'Comfy are we? 'Got yourself some new threads I see,' Caz commented sarcastically, having to shout a little to be heard over the warbling of the opera singers.

Rosie cocked her head and looked at Caz, the slight movement making her look like an unwound clockwork doll that had been nudged, to move one final click forward before coming to rest again in a stiff pose.

'What're you listening to?' she shouted, picking up the record sleeve that lay on Rosie's bed.

On the cover a man wearing a suit of white feathers was carrying a bird cage. *The Magic Flute* written in ornate black lettering on a pale blue background. The music got louder, the orchestra and a chorus of singers really belting it out before coming to a dramatic climax. On the ancient recording, the applause that followed sounded like crackling paper. Then the air was filled with the gentle pft of dust hitting the needle before the arm automatically rose and swung back, coming to rest. Rosie still hadn't responded to Caz's question.

'How're the legs?' said Caz.

'They don't hurt if I don't move them,' Rosie replied in a small far away voice.

Caz walked to the window and looked down on Lacy and Tink.

'Looks like mum's having fun outside with Lord Lacy. Shame you can't join them, but that would mean giving the game away. Still, must be getting a bit boring being stuck up here on your own.' Caz stretched her arms over her head and did a little playful gig around the room. 'It's such a lovely day, I thought I might go to the village and get an ice cream. I'd bring you one back, but it'll probably go all melty on the way.' She glanced at Rosie to see if this taunt had hit home. 'I'll just have to eat one for you.'

Rosie looked back at her calmly, refusing to be baited.

'Well, that's nice that you've come to cheer up your sister,' Mrs Dixon said, entering the room with a tray in hand.

'I thought she'd be a bit bored, not being able to get out and about.' Caz smiled brightly at Mrs Dixon, doing her concerned big sister act. 'It's sad to see her suffering so much.'

'Well, I've brought you both up a spot of lunch. Maybe you can eat it together. I'm afraid your clothes aren't dry yet, Catherine, so you'll just have to get by with what you're in for a while longer. How on earth you were planning to get your stuff clean, well I don't know. Anyway, we haven't got anything in your size.'

'I would have washed some things out in the sink with a bit of soap.'

Caz had hoped to impress Mrs Dixon with her resourcefulness, but instead the remark earned her a look of pity.

Mrs Dixon placed a pretty wicker tray down on Rosie's bedside table. It was loaded with a plateful of dainty sandwiches cut into triangles, four chocolate biscuits, grapefruit juice and a couple of apples. Caz wondered if the horrible dinner the night before had been on purpose, or if it was just that Mrs Dixon was only really good at making sandwiches.

'Well, tuck in,' Mrs Dixon said, straightening up, wincing slightly and placing her fists behind her back.

'Thank you,' said Rosie in her far away voice, leaning over and wincing dramatically herself as she took a sandwich.

Delicately cupping one hand under the sandwich to catch the crumbs as she raised it to her lips, she ate like a bird, each peck leaving behind a tiny crescent of neat teeth marks in the bread.

'I'm not very hungry, I just ate breakfast,' said Caz.

'No, you were dead to the world when I came up this morning. Does your mum usually let you stay up all hours?' said Mrs Dixon disapprovingly.

'I just couldn't sleep. I'm not used to sleeping indoors or something. I kept hearing noises in the night,' said Caz blushing.

'I suppose it takes a bit of getting used to, the way this house moans and groans. But it's nothing to worry about. We don't have ghosts. I ought to know, spent so much time up here on my own while Ronnie was away at school and with his Lordship overseas... It's not right that this place has been so empty for so long. We used to have lovely parties.' Mrs Dixon sat down on a chair and fixed her eyes on Rosie.

'What kind of parties?' Rosie asked, pursing her lips and fluttering her eyelashes.

'Fancy dress, used to have one every year. People came from all over. You ask Ronnie about it. Lady Lacy would help him pick out a costume.'

Rosie continued to delicately eat her sandwich, while Mrs Dixon looked at her, eyes misty with emotion. Caz selected a fish paste sandwich and munched it down herself.

'Is Ronnie around?' she asked when she'd done.

Mrs Dixon snapped out of it and turned to Caz.

'I think he's in the library doing some studying. They make him work so hard in that school, poor love. I'm sure he'd love to take a break though.'

'I don't know where the library is.'

'I'll take you there. But is Rosie going to be okay up here on her own?'

'The doctor said plenty of rest, I don't want to tire her out,' replied Caz. 'She was listening to her record, I'll turn it over for her.'

Before going down she collected her Walkman and a few tapes she wanted to play to Ronnie, then followed Mrs Dixon along the corridor. Admiring the way her stocky body filled her dress, Caz felt the embarrassing urge to bury her head in this woman's comfortable looking flesh. It made her feel both faintly awkward and happy to be around her.

'Actually, Mrs Dixon, the doctor seems to think that Rosie isn't really sick. It's probably psychomatic.'

'Psychomatic? What's that?'

'It means that it's all in her head,' said Caz. 'I think she wanted to be sick so that we wouldn't leave. She's been really weird lately. Well, she's always weird, but she's been weirder than ever since we got here.'

'Don't you think you ought to give her the benefit of the doubt?'

'No, I'm just saying that like, well right the doctor says to leave her on her own and then she will snap out of it if she's play acting, we shouldn't give her too much attention. But mum and Mr Lacy, like yesterday they were making a big fuss of her and reading her stories and stuff, that's not what the doctor said.'

'That doctor can be a bit hard hearted you know. He was really rough with Ronnie when he had the measles once. Besides, your mum's the one who knows what's best for your sister.'

'Does she?' said Caz.

Mrs Dixon's bosom heaved and she let out a huge sigh.

'I'm not going to say nothing against your mum. She has her way of doing things and you best do what she tells you. You're not really big enough to understand everything and I know you think you are, but I assure you, you're not.'

Caz knew that Mrs Dixon disapproved of her mum, so it was disappointing that she wouldn't be drawn into slagging her off. They reached the ground floor and turned down a corridor Caz hadn't been down before. At the end was a huge oak door.

'Ronnie's in there. Mind you tell him his lunch'll be ready in 30 minutes,' said Mrs Dixon, before turning away.

The padded door thumped shut behind her flooding the room with a suffocating silence. Despite the warmth of the day outside, the library was chilly so that Caz, wearing just a t-shirt and jeans, had to wrap her arms around herself. Holding out her hand, the wrinkles of light that filtered through the frosted windowpanes made her mottled skin look as if it had been submerged.

Dressed in a pure wool cardigan over a brushed cotton t-shirt, Ronnie sat studying at the far end of a large wooden table. His well-conditioned hair fell forward and gleamed attractively in the soft light. Caz looked down at her freckled dirty feet encased in cheap sparkly jellybean sandals and smelt the stale scent of sweat rising up from the armpits of her crumpled t-shirt.

'Hello,' he greeted her from under his hair, not looking up from his work.

'Your mum says your lunch will be ready in 30 minutes.'

Ronnie did not respond and continued to write. Caz sat down in a chair that squeaked as she eased herself into it.

'So, I hear you'll be staying with us for a while,' Ronnie said finally, still not looking her way.

Caz wondered if he was mad that she had left him on the lawn that morning without saying goodbye.

'Just till Rosie's legs are better. Mr Lacy says mum can help him with his cataloguing, so it's not charity or anything.'

Ronnie looked up at her, eyes glinting. 'But I'm doing the cataloguing.' A slick smile spread across his face. 'Oh, I get it.'

'What?'

The room fell silent again and Ronnie went back to writing in his book. Caz's heart thumped, should she leave? What did he 'get?' Was he thinking that they were a charity case, that Lacy was letting her mum think she was paying her way?

A dry sound of tiny footsteps slowly approaching made Caz spin round startled, but it was only the sound of a grandfather clock ticking off the seconds. Ronnie looked up and frowned at her to let her know she was distracting him. She would get something to read. He couldn't complain if she didn't disturb him.

She looked at the rows of books. The shelves were groaning with large tomes that had boring sounding titles embossed in gold on their spines. Titles like, *A Commentary and Review of Montesque's Spirit of Laws*. Having no idea who Montesque was, she thought it was probably not worth her while reading a commentary on his works. The next book she reached for at random was *The Works of Vicesimus Knox*. This brutal Victorian-sounding name did not appeal either, so she replaced the heavy volume.

'I doubt they'll be anything to interest you,' Ronnie said, not deigning to look up from his work.

She ignored him and continued to search for something. When she finally arrived at Shakespeare, she decided that this would have to do. She'd seen the movie of Romeo and Juliet with her grandma on the telly last year, it had been okay. But the volume was high up, which meant she would have to fetch the stairs.

The ladder was on rails so that when she moved it, it squeaked as it ran along the floor. Ronnie sighed at the grating noise. Finally arriving at the stack she needed, she began to climb. Even with the ladder, she had to stand on tip toe to reach the volume. She grabbed at it and it sprang from the shelf, falling with a fatal thump on the floor.

Ronnie jumped to his feet and examined the volume for damage.

'I couldn't reach, so...'

'Why didn't you ask me? I could have got it down for you.' He held the book close to his chest as if comforting the victim of a violent attack. 'Hadn't you better leave before you break anything else?'

CHAPTER FIFTEEN

With the hot road empty of traffic, the hedgerows buzzed all the louder with insect life. Caz lashed out at anything that got too close, arms flailing ineffectually through the air. But apart from the odd accidental collision, the insects were indifferent to her: bumblebees buzzed sleepily around wild blossoms and fat bluebottles hovered over piles of fresh manure. There was nobody to see her crying. She didn't want anyone to see her crying. Heavy with the stench of weeds and cow shit, waves of heat rolled up from the melting tarmac, making her feel nauseous every time she drew breath between heaving sobs.

A bee lay on the burning surface of the road, its delicate veined wings still, slightly crumpled. Caz knelt and touched its quivering body with her finger. It was soft, furry. She stood back up and stomped on it, feeling a satisfying crunch under the sole of her sandal. The action seemed to distract her long enough to bring her tears under control. Still sniffing, throat swollen from crying hard, she bent down to the stream by the side of the road and splashed cold water onto her puffy face, before straightening up.

Tink would eventually notice that she'd gone missing and then she'd be sorry. It was a good thing she was getting away from Upton Park. It was way too creepy in there with Rosie acting like a Stepford child. She put her earphones on and pressed play, then continued her journey away from the manor.

After about 15 more minutes, she reached a little church that appeared to be on the outskirts of the village. She needed somewhere quiet to sit. The old churchyard seemed ideal. Wandering around the crumbling stones in the graveyard, she wondered where the fresh graves were. Perhaps nobody had died in a long while; they had simply vanished into thin air just like Sophie had done. She sat down on the warm roots of a giant tree, resting with her back against the trunk and her face to the sun.

With her Walkman on, it took her awhile to notice that somebody was standing over her, blocking out the sunlight. She opened her eyes and saw the shadowy form of a little girl haloed in light. The sun shone over the girl's shoulder so Caz, squinting, couldn't make out her face. This girl was the same height as Rosie. Caz removed her earphones and pressed pause.

'What yous listening to?' enquired the girl, voice clogged with country burr.

'The Cure.'

'Gis us a go,' the girl said, holding out her hand.

She smelt terrible.

'No.'

The girl began to scratch her elbow, a huge scab coming off in her dirty fingers. She nibbled at it thoughtfully then turned her attention back to Caz.

'My brother's just round the corner. He'll make you give it if I calls him.'

Caz shrugged, this was probably an empty threat, but she stood up, ready to leg it if necessary. Now she could get a better look at the girl. She was about the same age as Rosie with the kind of long straight brown hair Caz usually envied, but the state of it, greasy and speckled with dandruff, disgusted her. She almost gagged on the scent of BO gone rancid.

'Yous not from round here are yous. Never seen you before.'

'We're staying at Upton Park,' said Caz in her best BBC accent.

'Oooh, posh is you?' The girl kicked the side of a gravestone with the toe of a grubby white shoe.

'We're guests of Lord Lacy.'

'You wants to watch out you does. My mum won't let me play near there, she says they can't prove nothing 'cause he's rich.'

'Can't prove what?'

'He's a dark one says my mum. Little girls aint safe with him.'

'You live in the village?'

The girl nodded.

'What's your name?'

The girl sniffed and looked away as if worried about revealing her identity.

'Greer. Greer Price,' she said quietly.

Caz stepped forward and looked Greer in the eye. 'I'll make sure I mention it to Lord Lacy. Let him know who's been spreading rumours about him. He doesn't like gossips. Did you know he's got a room full of Japanese swords? They're dead sharp. Good for chopping little girls up into small pieces with.'

The girl's gormless-looking mouth twisted, emitting an injured howl, as if she'd been punched. As Caz watched her stumble away, she felt triumphant. These yokels were loads easier to fend off than the kids on site. But she couldn't risk hanging round there any longer; the girl's big brother might really be nearby.

******

It was getting late when she made her way back to the mansion. Her elongated shadow flung slightly ahead of her, flickering over the hedgerows to the right. On her left the sun loomed large and red over a field of stubble. Shredding the peace of the evening with their rasping cries, a few crows were perched on a rusty iron gate. As she drew near, they fell silent. She felt nervous in their presence. Walking past their territory, she got the feeling that things could turn nasty.

She ought to have run at them flapping her arms and shouting, but she'd had enough confrontation for the day. Instead, she tried to ignore them and walked at a calm measured pace. They observed her as she passed, jewelled eyes glinting. When she reached the path that led through the woods to Upton Park, she turned off and began to run, stumbling on roots and skittering on rocks, inches away from a bad fall.

She arrived, breathless, back at the manor, her shoes squeaking on the stone floor making a nasty noise that she could feel in her teeth. She removed them and made her way through to the back of the house, leaving a trail of sweaty footprints that slowly faded behind her, then vanished, like ghost tracks.

'It would upset the girls, especially Caz.'

The door to the room where Tink and Lacy were working was open a touch, allowing her to listen in on their conversation. Though she could only see a thin triangular slice of the study, she could hear their voices clearly. Pressing her body close to the door, she could just about make out Lacy, sitting down at the table, intently looking across at what she assumed was her mother. She tried to breathe quietly.

'And you too, no?' queried Lacy.

'Yes, and me too. He just dropped off the radar and didn't get in touch for years. I'm still so angry. And you know, you can't know what he's like, he comes in and everyone falls for him, for his bullshit. It's like he's got this really vibrant energy, so that everything is buzzing when he's around, but it's also really disruptive, it messes people up.'

'Hope you don't mind me saying this, but doesn't that sound a bit like someone else who left recently?' Lacy said making a note on a pad in front of him.

'You mean Chris? No, but the thing is see, is that Chris right, he's really upfront. He's always said that he's not ready to be a dad. He keeps his distance, they know where they stand.'

'Riiiggghhht.' Lacy drew out the word, interjecting it with doubt. He began to push something small around the table with the tip of his pencil, like a scientist examining an unusual specimen.

'Caz at least does, that's why she's always so angry with him. She's so wary of getting hurt, even though I know she likes Chris, she won't let him get close. Perhaps it's a good thing, but it can't be healthy for her in the long run. She got very strange when her dad left.'

'I'm afraid she hasn't warmed to me yet.' He smiled and looked in the direction of the door.

Caz stayed put. Had he seen her? It was dark out in the hallway, there was no way she was visible.

Her mum continued, intent on her own monologue, 'But Rosie, well you saw how quickly she took to you, she's the complete opposite of Caz. She doesn't have any barriers, which is a worry. But you know, she really can sense if someone is giving off a bad vibe and stays away. It's pretty spooky really, I mean this one guy, we all liked him in the squat but Rosie wouldn't go near him. Anyway one day the police turn up and it turns out he's on the run from Ireland for keeping weapons for the IRA.'

Caz wondered if she was talking about Paul, the scary Irish drunk with the boggly eyes? Everyone else talked to him because they were frightened he'd deck them if they didn't.

'Rosie is a very sensitive child. That's a blessing and a curse, I expect she's very artistic.' Lacy laid down his pencil and moved out of view, towards Tink.

'Yes, very, she's always scribbling stories or drawing.'

'It's hard to protect someone so sensitive. Especially on your own and with so many...' Lacy searched for a tactful phrase. 'Interesting characters around.'

Tink was silent, Caz strained to hear what was going on.

'Back are we?'

Startled, Caz span around and came face to face with Mrs Dixon.

'Won't ever hear no good of yourself,' she said loudly.

'Sorry?' Caz asked for clarification.

Mrs Dixon lowered her voice and put her face up so close that Caz could almost feel the heat radiating out of her broken capillaries.

'Listening in.'

She straightened and then barged past Caz into the study.

'Dinner's on the table,' she announced.

'Mrs Dixon, you are a lifesaver. We're absolutely famished.'

'I found this one loitering nearby.'

Tink shot Caz a concerned look and Caz looked away out the window.

'You don't mind if I send her up with the sandwiches for young Rosie, do you?'

'No, that would be perfect, the girls can eat together. Tell Rosie I'll be up soon to tuck her in,' said Tink.

******

Caz banged up the stairs, trying to make as much noise as possible, to let them all know how angry she was. The soft carpets and sombre walls swallowed up the sound, smothering her rage. They could talk about her behind her back, but they weren't even worried about where she'd been. As Lacy drew closer and closer to Tink and Rosie, she felt like she was drifting further and further away, becoming less substantial, almost transparent, like a ghost drifting along the corridors. Perhaps she'd start meeting the other phantoms who were quietly haunting this place.

Nobody had turned on the hall lights, so that she was forced to make her way back through the gloom. All day her mind had buzzed with static, and now as the light began to fade, something seemed to squirm at the edges of her vision in the pooling darkness, like a TV channel that wasn't tuned in properly.

She found Rosie comatose, breathing heavily and twitching in response to unseen threats. On the duvet in front of her was the little red notebook that she used as a diary. Caz didn't hesitate, but seized the book and took it into her own room.

Written on the inside cover in a sprawling anarchic hand: *Rosie Thompson, Rainbowe House, Kentish Ton, London, Engeland, THE EARTH, THE SOLER SISTEM, THE UNIVARSE.*

Though each paragraph stared out neatly, as the writer's excitement grew, so did the size of the letters, breaking out from the bounds on the printed line so that they spilled over and merged with the text above, making it hard going trying to decipher any meaning.

Flipping forward to the latest entry, she began to read. *Caz ses now I am sik I cant find the gril in the forest but in mi drem the girl came to talk to me and sed it waz ok for uz to stay she is about mi age so we undertand each other I am angre wiv Caz she always spoils tings and has no imagination. <u>SHE WIL BE SORY SOON</u>!!!*

CHAPTER SIXTEEN

The morning gleamed with promise and Caz glowered back with barely concealed rage. She'd tried to thank Mrs Dixon for the freshly laundered clothes she'd found at the end of her bed, but instead was loaded up with jug of orange juice and sent packing out across the green turf to where the others were sitting.

Not wanting to meet anyone's eye, she instead stared off at a plane flying high above their heads. It flashed silver, stitching a short white seam that gradually unravelled backwards into the brilliant blue sky. Tiny gold spirals flared away from the tail of the vapour cloud, burning her retina and making her eyes water. She'd hardly slept again and could barely stand the bright light.

The breakfast things were half demolished. The tablecloth scattered liberally with debris of torn croissant and stained with globs of jam and butter. Tink leaned back in her chair, ankles crossed, legs stretched out before her, hands clasped over her belly with a satisfied look on her face. Rosie was leaning in close to Mr Lacy, telling him all about her friend Zuza, the crocodile, who lived in an electric power station. When Caz slammed the jug of orange juice down on the table and drew up a chair, the charming little monologue died on Rosie's pouting lips.

'We're celebrating,' Lacy announced.

'Oh.' Caz picked up a croissant and placed it on her plate.

'Rosie's legs seem to be improving. At the least the pain is abating somewhat,' said Lacy, patting Rosie's hand.

'I walked a little bit, but then I got tired, didn't I? Maybe I won't need to go to the hopital,' she whispered to Lacy.

'Well, we don't want to send you to the HOSpital either, so we're all glad you're feeling better,' said Lacy.

'It's really miraculous, if you think about it, this sudden recovery,' said Caz, imitating Lacy's posh voice, but not looking him in the eye.

'It is brilliant is what it is,' Tink put in, in a tone that was meant to sound threatening.

'It's early days yet and she's still fragile, but this morning, as you can see, we were able to move her downstairs,' Lacy said, as if he hadn't detected the sarcasm in Caz's voice.

The pair of them beamed at each other, no doubt picturing the feeble invalid smiling bravely through a veil of tears as she struggled to overcome her fictitious ailments. Caz applied butter and jam to her croissant and took a bite, careful to lean over her plate so as not to make a mess. She let the silence really settle in as she munched slowly.

'Chris is coming back today, isn't he?' she said, after swallowing down the first mouthful.

'Well, I was wanting to talk to you about that love, you see, he called yesterday, and we've decided that it's best if we stay here. Rosie really needs more time to recuperate, and Rupert is happy to have us. There's several weeks of summer holiday left, so I thought it'd be nice for us to spend them here. You didn't really like being out in the van, did you? I mean it was so cramped and you and Rosie were always bickering, this way you get your own space. Rosie's really keen on the idea,' Tink trailed off.

'Are you alright love?'

She couldn't seem to get used to the blinding light and, to stop her eyes from watering, Caz had been pressing her palms against them while Tink had been talking. She took them away and nodded her head, then glared across the table at the traitor. They'd argued before, been screaming that they hated each other, but it was different this time, it was like she was seeing her sister in a new light and realising that she was a total stranger. She thought about the threat she'd read in Rosie's diary, *SHE WIL BE SORY SOON*. Was that the kind of thing a normal sister would write?

'We are going to see the magic operwa in Birwingham,' she said, lisping the way she used to do when she was younger.

'The Magic Flute. You remember we listened to it on the roof that day when we had a picnic, love. Mr Lacy heard it was on nearby. You'll love that won't you? We can get dressed up,' said Tink.

'And you'll get the chance to spend more time with Ronnie. I know you two have been as thick as thieves. It'll be fantastic for him to have someone his own age around.' Lacy picked up the teapot and poured her a cup.

'Have some fruit Caz, it's really delicious.' Tink bit into a plum, juice squirting down her chin, leaving a gruesome spatter pattern on the white cotton tablecloth.

'What will we do with you, didn't anyone teach you table manners, you little savage?' Lacy leant over and wiped away the juice with a napkin.

Tink laughed loudly at this comment and Caz shot her a look of disdain.

'You said you'd show me the butterfwies,' said Rosie, regaining Lacy's attention by lisping in an overly sweet voice.

'Of course, I did, didn't I? Do you think you'll be okay with me lifting you up the stairs again?'

Rosie nodded and held out her hands for Lacy, letting herself be lifted out of the chair and carried back to the house.

Caz and Tink watched them leave, neither of them saying a word. She should say something about the missing girl, about the swords, about what the girl in the village had said to her…

'What's up sugar pop?'

Caz gave her mum a weak smile. 'Nothing, just missing grandma and granddad.'

'I know love, I miss them too,' Tink said, sleepily, leaning her head back and basking in the sunlight.

'Maybe we could give them a call tonight?'

Tink opened an eye and looked at Caz, stretched, yawned, and then sat up in her chair. 'Well, why don't we wait till Rosie's properly back on her feet? They're getting on a bit, so we don't want to get them worried over nothing. You know what grand-dad is like, he'll be racing down the M1 before you know it and we don't want him to be driving with his hip. Let's not bother them with our little drama for the time being. I reckon we can handle this for now, don't you? Besides, this is an adventure!'

With this, Tink got up from the table, leaving the mess behind her.

Caz stayed behind. She felt weak, as if the bright light had drained all the strength out of her body. Her eyes had stopped watering, but now she wasn't even able to move. She stared at a wasp that was buzzing angrily round the jam jar in front of her but couldn't bring herself to move further away. She had to do something. Everything was coming apart. What was wrong with her? Why didn't she do something?

When she finally jumped up it didn't seem as if she had made the decision to stand herself. She'd been sat there ages willing her body to move, but as if someone else had flicked a switch, she was set in motion again. The thought that she wasn't in control of her own movements frightened her. Was she beginning to suffer the same fate as Rosie? Why hadn't she said anything? It was like Upton Park was some bog they'd got stuck in and the more she tried to escape, the more deeply she sank into the mire.

She shook her head and got to work collecting the plates and running them down to the kitchen. Returning with a wet sponge, she placed the butter and jam on the paving stones, shook the cloth out and began sponging off the worst of the stains. Cleaning stuff always made her feel better.

'What on earth are you up to?'

For such a large lady, it was amazing the way Mrs Dixon managed to sneak up on people.

'I just wanted to help out with the mess,' Caz said, gripping the dripping sponge.

'You won't get them stains off with that, you might as well be trying to shift that great blueberry splodge off old Gorby's bonce.' The severe expression on Mrs Dixon's face melted into a smile.

Caz, chastised, looked up in relief.

'I took the plates in. I was going to go back in a minute and wash them up.'

'Now aren't you a treasure. But you do know I get paid for this, I don't do it out of the goodness of my heart.'

'I want to do it though.' Caz stood her ground.

'Oh, well then, I best let you take care of it all then and I can relax and have a cup of tea.'

******

In the half light of the submerged kitchen, they waited for the tea to brew. The mantelpiece was overpopulated with porcelain figurines of shepherdesses, fairies, and forest creatures, their frozen faces looking up pleadingly at Caz. She didn't mind this kind of stuff, it was what old people liked, but something about it really seemed to drive her mum over the edge. One quiet Sunday afternoon in Radlett, the kind of peace descended on her grandparent's house that tended to make Tink really lose her shit.

'They're just things, why do you want to like burden yourself with objects?' Tink had said to grandma.

She'd been seated cross-legged on the floor, wearing a pair of billowing cotton trousers that granddad said she must have pinched off Aladdin. Tink had always tried her utmost to look out of place in the upholstered floral cosiness of her parent's lounge.

'Of course they're things, they're my things. I like having them. They're not a burden, they give me a little lift and god knows I need that these days. When you finally move into your own place, you'll understand.' Her grandma let this remark hit home and continued to dust her 'trinkets.'

This was a heavy hint. They'd been on the council waiting list for a few months by then.

'You want this to define you?' Tink had picked up a weeping Pierrot in a pastel harlequin suit.

'It's pretty, it cheers me up and if you don't like it, you can go and stay elsewhere madam.'

When Tink smashed it against the fireplace, she had looked as stunned as the rest of them.

Mrs Dixon laid a plateful of lumpen cakes in front of Caz. The raisins in the dough had burnt solid in the oven so that Caz was afraid that she might break a tooth if she bit into one.

'I like my little knickknacks, they keep me company now that Mr Dixon has passed on. It's been a little lonely since Ronnie went away to school, not that I'm complaining mind.' Mrs Dixon poured the tea and sat down.

'My grandma collects figurines too. I help her dust them sometimes.' If Tink had been there, she would have called Caz a 'goody two shoes' for saying this.

'Do you see your grandma much then?' Mrs Dixon's face squished up with concern, her little green eyes almost disappearing in her ham pink flesh.

'Not since we moved to London. Mum and grandma tend to rub each other up the wrong way, but I liked living there. Mum said that living on an estate is really boring, but it's okay. It's like everything normal makes my mum really really mad. So we have to do everything different because it's an adventure, I see that but, like with sofas, okay, my mum says we'll get lazy if we sit on sofas all the time. In the squat, we always sat on the floor on cushions, they're all crazy for sitting on the floor. She thinks that if you get too comfortable you miss out on stuff or something. Like there's something really bad about sitting in a nice chair.'

'Well, she's certainly getting very comfortable here,' murmured Mrs Dixon into her tea. But she looked at Caz and her cross expression softened, 'I certainly appreciate the help this morning. To tell you the truth, I've been rushed off my feet since Lord Lacy got back, especially now he's spending more time here. Not that I'm complaining, god knows I'm happy to have him back, I was beginning to think he might never be coming back from Japan.'

She pushed the plateful of unappetising cakes towards Caz, who picked one up and raised it to her mouth, then lowered it as if she'd just remembered something important.

'What was he doing in Japan?' Caz picked one of the scorched raisins out of the heavy piece of pastry, almost breaking a nail in the process.

'Seems to me like he was getting as far away from here as possible, and who can blame him. Along with Lady Lacy, the rest of the staff just upped sticks. He never was charged with anything in court, but they all took it upon themselves to be judge and jury.'

Caz glanced at Mrs Dixon, heart thumping. Now was the time to ask.

'Because Sophie disappeared?'

Mrs Dixon's face glowed a brighter shade of red, the filaments of hair that stuck out from her head looked as if they might start sending off sparks. Caz looked away. She felt like all the atoms inside her were agitated, wriggling around like on a blank TV screen, breaking up.

'Ronnie told me about Sophie,' she whispered. 'He seemed really upset about it.'

To dampen Mrs Dixon's anger Caz bit off a lump of cake and chewed, almost dislocating her jaw as she did so. She made an appreciative noise and set the cake back down again.

'She was the most adorable thing. I don't think he'll ever get over it and what they said in the papers was a crime itself. I suppose you're too young to remember any of it, but we do, like it was yesterday. About this time of year too, so it cuts particularly hard.

'I know he's a funny one, but it's only shyness. I have a cousin just the same, people always seem to take him the wrong way, but it's just that he doesn't mix well with most people. He had all those parties for Lady Lacy. They said it was suspicious that they couldn't find him at his own party, but I told them, I used to catch him at it before, sneaking off. One time, he was skulking around in the cellar, said he's looking for a bottle of wine, gone for nearly an hour from his own dinner party.

'The papers were all nice at first, slithering around here, saying if we cooperate it's our best chance of getting her back. But then they laid into him, started saying how nobody could account for Lord Lacy's movements for some of that night. He loved that little girl, he would never do anything to harm her.' Mrs Dixon's plump hands gripped her mug tightly. Scrubbed raw, Caz noticed they were covered in scratches and burns as if she had really been fighting tooth and nail to protect Lacy's reputation.

'And he always stood by me, when my husband died and I was at my wits end, he told me to put my feet up, that there'd always be a place for me here. He gave me paid leave for one month. Since then, he took an interest in Ronnie and when he saw that he was so bright, he organized for him to go to Ardingly like he was his own. Of course, there'll always be a limit to just how much we could mingle, though that all seems to have gone out the window with your mum. Not that I'm not grateful for what Mr Lacy's done for him.' Mrs Dixon took a bite out of her cake. She bit down hard and began chewing, saliva-wet dough sloshing noisily around her mouth.

'So, you had a party when she went missing?' Caz blew on her tea and took a sip, the cup shaking in her hands as she lifted it up to her mouth.

'It was some charity thing. A ball. Of course, Sophie wanted to go, screamed blue murder. They reckon that's why she went to run away. They found her case, near where we lived, you know, the round house, the little red monkey case that he bought her from Florence. It was packed with an orange, a pair of knickers and that rag doll she loved so much. So, I suppose she must have been thinking of running away. But why did she leave the case?' Mrs Dixon was looking at the figurines as she said this, as if they might give her an answer. They stared back at her with tragic eyes.

'It's that case that makes me think that someone must have took her. She was a little poppet. Always playing with Ronnie. They were so close, it did hit him hard you know, he's never been the same since. None of us has. I couldn't stay in that house any longer. I kept thinking that any minute she might come out of the trees. You see why we got such a shock then when Rosie turned up, like she's Sophie herself come back to us.'

Caz stood up, leaving the cake on the table in front of her. Felt the whole room tilt, everything became unstable, the porcelain figures on the window tipping forward, about to smash on the ground. Caz had the insane urge to get it over with, to dash them to pieces herself. Though she'd swallowed the mouthful of cake, it felt like it was still lodged in her throat, choking her. It was hot and she was having trouble breathing. She gulped down the scalding tea, trying to think of an excuse to leave.

'I think I left my Walkman outside,' she said.

Mrs Dixon looked up at her surprised, then looked at the uneaten cake. Caz was already at the door, trying to get away from the nasty looking thing. She turned the handle and threw a wave to Mrs Dixon before running off up the stairs.

Outside, Bill was bent down on his knees with a trowel, weeding the flowerbeds. Hearing her footsteps on the gravel driveway, he raised his head and looked at her as she approached on wobbly legs.

'Hello,' she said, brightly.

He dipped his head a touch, barely acknowledging her and went back to his task. A faint whirring noise started up, but when Caz looked around to find the source, she couldn't see anything. She felt weak, her legs shaking. She was barely able to stand up and her heart thumped fast, filling her throat, making her feel as if she might choke. She was only able to make it halfway across the lawn before she had to sit down. Turning back to the house, she saw that Bill was watching her. She waved weakly, but he didn't respond or look away. The world seemed to tilt forward again, and she dug her fingers into the unkempt grass, trying to get a secure grip.

She had to get away before it was too late, but the horrible thought hit her that it was already too late. Somehow during that night with Ronnie, she had opened a door into another world and something nasty had slipped through and was trying to take shape here. Her fingers were now in her hair, tugging harder and harder, as if she could make the thoughts stop if she yanked hard enough.

The familiar gesture brought her back to herself and she took a deep breath, picked up a daisy, and began to carefully pull off its petals one by one with her shaking fingers, all the while singing to comfort herself. *Daisy, daisy, give me your answer do. I'm half crazy all for the love of you. It won't be stylish marriage. I can't afford a carriage, but you'll look sweet upon the seat of a bicycle made for two.*

Gradually her breathing slowed and her heartbeat softened until all she wanted to do was to lie down on the grass. She looked back up to the house. Bill was still there but had turned his attention back to the flowerbeds. She got up and made her way into the woods. She just needed some sleep. If she could get into the round house, she could curl up on the sofa for a bit.

Caught in whirling currents of warm air, the canopy of leaves sighed as it rose and fell above her head. Light fluttered between her outstretched fingers, reminding her of a silent film she'd seen where dancing figures flickered light and dark like candle flames about to be extinguished. Now the terror she'd felt in the kitchen had faded, her head was fuzzy and vague. She felt a strong desire to just lie down on the dry earth.

She emerged in the familiar clearing and walked toward the house. To get in she'd have to punch out the cardboard they'd used to seal up the window and lift the latch by sticking her hand through the jagged pane of glass. But just in case, she tried the doorknob. The door opened.

Ronnie looked even more surprised than she was.

'What are you doing here?' he asked sharply.

Confused and sleepy, Caz didn't know how to answer. Why

was she there?

'I'm just tidying up a bit, for mum,' he said, changing his tone and answering his own question.

She noticed he was carrying a blue plastic carrier bag in his hand. Almost as soon as she had time to register this, he put his arms behind his back, hiding the bag from view. Wearing a faded Stone Roses t-shirt that hung loosely on his slender frame, he leaned against the doorframe and watched her. Out in the sunshine, she felt so sleepy that it was almost impossible to stay standing up. She wobbled over to the rusted metal roller that stood by the side of the house and sat down.

'It's covered in slugs,' Ronnie remarked.

'Can't I go in and sit down then?'

'Sorry,' he said, seeming at first to refuse. 'Of course.'

Inside, it was clear that he hadn't been tidying up. A boom box sat on the table along with an ashtray and a stubbed-out roach. The room smelt strongly of hash. Caz sat down on the sofa and tried not to look at the hideous drawings on the wall.

'Fancy a spliff? I found some decent sized butts in the ashtray left over from the party,' Ronnie said, picking up the charred butt of a joint.

'No.'

He shrugged and lit the thing up, choking as he inhaled. 'What's up with you? You mad at me or something?'

She looked at him. He tucked his fringe under his ear and smiled simply at her. His hair must have grown longer, because for once it stayed in place. She was so sleepy, it was hard to find the right words to explain why she was mad, so she was forced to limply reply, 'Nothing, I'm just, you know.'

Her words trailed off and she stared up at the swirling blue haze that hung above their heads. Warped faces appeared in the curling smoke and just as quickly slipped away, as if they were trying unsuccessfully to take physical form. Scared that if she stared for long enough something would emerge, Caz sat up and focused instead on Ronnie.

'You got the album?' she gestured to his t-shirt.

'Uh, yeah, but it's just a tape recording.'

'Can you put it on?' she said, putting her feet up on the table and scrunching further down into the comfy sofa.

Ronnie got up from the armchair and opened a cupboard, pulling out a battered metal biscuit tin. After extracting the right tape, he replaced the lid and stored the tin back where he'd got it from. She'd wanted to ask permission to rifle through his collection, but already feeling like she'd intruded into his private world, she held back.

After slotting the tape into the player, he continued sucking on the dog end. A swirl of distorted guitars began to sear through the dead hiss of blank sound, before the familiar bass line kicked in. Expertly holding the joint between his thumb and finger, Ronnie inhaled and winced, then coughed violently. Caz nuzzled her cheek against the worn velvety fabric of the sofa.

I don't have to sell my soul... Ronnie mouthed along with Ian Brown, puffing out smoke as he sang.

Embarrassed, her eyes were drawn back to the shifting patterns in the smoke.

You adore me, you adore me, sang Ian Brown.

The sofa dipped as he sat down beside her, and when he put his arm round her, her insides seemed to dip too, like when a lift suddenly comes to a stop. He leant over to kiss her, his face so close that she couldn't focus on it. Their lips pressed together, and she smelt Tic Tacs on his breath and fabric softener from his clothes.

'I just noticed that your freckles are the same colour as your hair. It's such a bright colour, not quite natural, like cheesy puffs.' He giggled. 'GOD, cheesy puffs would be sooo great right now, don't you think?'

Angry, she tried to pull her hand away, but he held on firmly. With the other hand he picked up the spliff and went back to smoking.

'So, when is what's his face, you know, that skanky guy coming back to collect you?' he asked, face contorted as he blew out more smoke.

148

'He's not. Mum says we're going to stay here with Mr Lacy.'

'No shit.' His hand tightened around hers. 'When did this happen?'

'She just told me this morning.'

Ronnie released her from his grip and sat forward so that his face was hidden from her.

'I don't want to be rude right, but Lacy creeps me out,' she said. 'Do you know what I mean?'

Ronnie didn't reply.

'I was actually wondering if you could help me, cause I want to like get out of here?' Stupidly her tone went up, like she was asking a question.

'I want to go back to London with Rosie, go back and stay with grandma and granddad, but I can't even do that without any money and I don't have any. I mean I've got three quid and that's literally it.'

Ronnie stopped the tape and continued to sit hunched over. The house creaked, as if straining in the grip of their uncomfortable silence.

'You want me to give you money?' he finally replied.

'No, I just thought you might know how I could get some. I could pay you back,' she said contradicting herself.

'I'm skint.'

'It's just everything is so weird.' Caz felt her eyes filling up with tears. 'I mean, first the doll, then Rosie's legs don't work, it's like she's different, and Mr Lacy hates me…'

She was crying, her head against the soft cotton fabric of Ronnie's t-shirt. He stroked her hand with one pale finger, a robotic gesture that reminded her of Lacy's nervous thumb ticking away. She had made him uncomfortable. She stood to get up, but Ronnie took her by the wrist and pulled her back onto the sofa. Now they had kissed he seemed to think he was free to push and pull her around.

'So, you need to get back to your grandparents. How much do you need?'

Caz shrugged. 'About 50 quid maybe.'

'I think I know how you can get that, but it's not going to be easy, you'll have to go back into the south wing.'

CHAPTER SEVENTEEN

The van slalomed up the driveway and skidded too late to a halt, chewing two strips of perfectly manicured lawn up with its tires. Chris was the first to emerge, spilling out of the driver's door and stumbling around, his string bean frame seeming to have lost all means of support, so that he was buffeted about like a ball of tumbleweed.

'He's completely shitfaced,' Ronnie remarked with delight.

Baz, emerging from the other side, was relatively stable. He removed a packet of fags from his shirt pocket and offered one to Chris. Resembling a pair of high priests performing an elaborate ritual, they lit up with slow, deliberate movements.

'It's the wrong way round,' Caz remarked as she neared the van.

Chris had been so engrossed in trying to light up the filter of his fag, that he hadn't noticed their approach. He looked up, taking a few seconds to focus his bloodshot eyes on her.

'Cazster! Great to see ya!' He enfolded her with gangly limbs, so that her nose was pressed up against his crumpled t-shirt. The sweat-stiffened fabric emitted a scent so potent that she almost fell to the ground. Baz tried to throw his arms around her next, but she swiftly stepped back and avoided his sad canine eyes.

'This is Ronnie.'

Chris grabbed Ronnie's hand.

'My MAAAAN!' he shouted, over enthusiastically.

'How are you doing?' Ronnie asked.

'I won't lie to you mate, I've been better.'

Baz put a comforting hand on Chris' wilting shoulders and he sagged a little further forward.

'What's it all about eh Cazziewaz? What's going on with your mum? She mad at me or what?'

'We jus wanna get stuff straight like,' interjected Baz. 'I tried to stop him but he was hell bent like. Couldnae let him go alone in that state,' Baz added with a serious look on his face.

'Where are they then?' Chris asked.

They all looked up at the house. Now that the morning sun had passed over, the façade was once again frowning in shadow. As they stared up, Rupert walked out of the door.

'Och, it's his lordship, come tae get rid o us commoners,' Baz muttered.

Hands in his pockets, Lord Lacy trotted gracefully down the steps. Wearing a pair of cords and a pin-striped white shirt, open at the neck with rolled up sleeves, he looked like he had dressed to impress his ordinariness upon his audience. He removed his right hand from his pocket and presented it to Chris.

Wobbling his head back and forth like a cobra under the influence of a snake charmer, Chris seemed so stunned by the unexpected presence of Lord Lacy, that he not so much declined the amicable gesture, but simply seemed to be unaware that anything was expected of him. Lacy cautiously withdrew the hand and replaced it in his pocket.

'I don't blame you for being rather peeved with me, I'd be bloody irritated if I were you. I suppose that's an understatement.' He turned and looked towards the forest. They all fell silent as a flock of birds whooshed over their heads, out towards the trees.

'It was nae very gallant of ye M'Lord,' Baz said eventually, speaking up for Chris, who still stood dumbstruck. They were quiet again. Caz noticed that tears had begun to fill Chris' eyes.

'I like…' he began, voice quavering. 'I like thought you were a safe bloke. I didn't think that like I was abandoning her and the kids. I left them in your CARE man.'

Caz felt deeply embarrassed for Chris. Why was he being such a drip?

'And I appreciate that you trusted me like that. It's just...' Lacy coughed 'things happen. We didn't want to hurt you. I rather took to you myself in fact. I really feel beastly.'

'Can I see her?' Chris blurted out.

'Are you really in any state? I mean, she's afraid you're going to a make a terrific scene.'

Chris looked down at his battered army boots. Any fight he had had in him had long since fled the scene. He flopped onto the stone steps, legs akimbo, head hanging down. Baz joined him on one side and flung an arm round him, accidentally flicking a light covering of ash onto his dishevelled curls. Lacy sat down on Chris' other flank.

A sharp finger jabbed into Caz's back. She turned to Ronnie, who was jerking his head towards the house. Reluctantly, she followed him inside. She couldn't think of any words to say in parting, and they hadn't noticed her departure anyway.

When they entered the hallway, Ronnie wheeled around, eyes glittering.

'I bet your mum is watching from the front of the house, I know my mum will be. This is like Christmas come early to her. She loves a bit of drama. We might as well sneak into the south wing now, while they're all distracted.'

Caz nodded. He took her hand again and they made their way up the stairs. Caz's legs felt unbelievably heavy as they went up, turning left at the top of the staircase towards the south wing. Ronnie was right, with everybody gathered at the front of the house, it would be easy to slip in without being noticed.

'I better keep watch near the entrance, so no one catches you coming out,' said Ronnie as they approached the door. 'I'll whistle if someone comes,'

Caz nodded and gulped, she could still feel the piece of cake that Mrs Dixon had given her bruising her throat. She opened the door and went in, closing it quickly behind her. A cold mouldy stench crawled down her throat as soon as she was inside. She shivered and hugged herself, then turned straight into the first room to her left.

The handle was stiff, but it gave and she found herself in a near pitch dark room that smelled of dust and spilled perfume. Rather than grope blind for a light switch, she decided to wait awhile for her eyes to adjust to the gloom. After a minute, the outline of a stool began to take shape. Squatting at her feet in the dark, it looked like it had been waiting to trip her up. A large four-poster bed dominated the room. Its heavy canopy had darkened with age so that the roses embroidered onto its fabric were hard to make out.

Along the wall closest to the door was a dressing table. A set of silver-backed combs gleamed in the dim light. Caz traced her fingers over the ornate raised patterns, fingertips gathering up dust as she did so. As she wiped them off on her dress, she caught sight of her shadowy reflection in the mirror, and started, a jagged stab of panic lacerating her chest, so that for a minute it was hard to breathe.

Forgetting that someone might see her, she made for the window and pulled open the heavy velvet curtains, sending out clouds of swirling dust that filled her lungs, leaving her spluttering and squinting in the light. The room overlooked the front lawn. It was early afternoon and the shadow cast by the great house was already creeping towards the fountain. Chris' van was still parked out in the driveway and though she couldn't see them, the indistinct voices of the men outside on the steps could be heard. Comforted by the sound, she pulled the curtains back together, leaving them open just enough to allow a trickle of light in.

Back at the dresser, she turned her attention to a small jewellery box. She opened it and found a small golden watch in the shape of a seashell nestled against a bed of funereal black velvet. She pocketed it and went back to the door. Opening it again, she went out into the corridor, but before she could get the door open, she heard Ronnie whistling.

She dived back into the room and resigned herself to waiting it out. Seeing as she was so sleepy, it would make sense just to take a nap. She crawled under the heavy-looking canopy of the four-poster bed. The mattress was ridiculously hard, but she nevertheless curled up and wrapped her arms around herself, listening to the indistinct voices of Chris and Lacy. Nobody was shouting and it sounded like Chris was doing most of the talking. She closed her eyes.

******

It was such a beautiful day and one of her and nana's favourite records was playing on the gramophone nearby. Rosie was wearing a white lacy dress Caz had never seen before, but she'd managed to smear juice all down the front. They were sitting out on the lawn together eating strawberries and cream.

Heaven, I'm in heaven, and my heart beats so that I can hardly speak, and I seem to find the happiness I seek, when we're out together dancing cheek to cheek.

Ronnie approached and held out his hand to her. She accepted and they began to spin around the fountain, laughing. She felt as if she were being lifted up and up, and before she realized it, was eight feet off the ground, treading air. Ronnie laughed and let go of her, drifting up into the sky as he did so, while she began to flail around, flapping her arms and legs in a desperate attempt to stay afloat. But it was no use; she came crashing down with a thud in the drawing room.

Mr Lacy, Tink, Mrs Dixon and Rosie were all sat down for dinner.

'The tutelux are looking splendid, don't you think my doorling?' gushed Tink, all posh.

'Why they can't take the shine off your fair browzoom my turtle dove,' replied Mr Lacy, kissing Tink's hand with a noisy slurping noise.

'Dinni dins papa,' shouted Rosie thumping her spoon on the domed lid of a silver platter.

'You do the honors Smithers,' cried Lacy.

Chris appeared at her side, dressed as a butler. He winked at her and placed a white gloved hand on the lid, removing it with a flourish. On the platter lay Sophie, eyes open wide, white dress splattered with what looked like blood. Mr Lacy took up a carving knife.

'Don't, it's only strawberry jam!' she tried to shout out, but it was too late, Mr Lacy was slicing her up with his knife.

'Leg or breast?' he enquired, spiking a bloody piece of flesh with a huge fork.

Caz attempted to scream, but found herself choked into silence, instead she ran away through the woods that had suddenly sprung up around her. The branches clawed at her and, as she made her way through, she began to become aware of something white, flashing through the trees behind her. It gained on her, and she stumbled, green flashes spotting her vision. She regained her footing only to run into a flock of crows. Their wings battered against her, and she tried to fight them off, bringing her fists up against claw and beak. Falling through thin air she hit the ground with a thump, waking up with her heart pounding in her ears, staring up at the canopy of the four-poster bed.

The room was darker, so at first she felt confused, wondering where she was. Then she remembered: she was hiding out. She tried to sit up, but found she wasn't able to move her body, and even when she attempted to clench and unclench her fists, her fingers remained rigid and motionless. A hot wave of panic swept over her paralyzed body. She was definitely awake, but she just couldn't seem to move. Her eyes had grown sharper, the irises expanding in her sleep to register more detail, so that she could now properly make out the design of the embroidery above her head and for the first time noticed a coat of arms with a bear and lion holding up a shield in the centre of swooping garlands of roses.

It was then that she became aware of someone was standing over her. She tried to say something but couldn't speak. She was locked in, about as capable of movement as the statues in the fountain outside. She couldn't even swallow and was having difficulty breathing. Was that Rosie, standing stock still, staring down at her? Somehow, she'd got hold of that doll again, and had the thing clasped to her chest. It was grinning inanely. Caz tried to struggle free but remained clamped to the bed. Her chest felt tight. Red and yellow spots began to appear in front of her eyes. Just as she was blacking out, she noticed that the girl had begun to smile.

She came to again in the same bed. Her limbs still felt heavy, and her mouth clogged. Had she been dreaming? She looked up and registered that the same coat of arms with the bear and lion holding up a shield was actually embroidered in the centre of the canopy above her head. Standing up, she went to the window. Chris' van had gone. How long had she been asleep for?

The smell of mould was like a fist down her dry throat when she went back into the corridor and stood listening at the door. Hearing nothing, she went out into the hall. There was no one there. She supposed Ronnie had got bored and left. She practically ran back to the other side of the house to their own bathroom, where she gulped down two glasses of tap water. Her face was puffy and swollen and her legs were wobbly underneath her.

Going back down the corridors towards the central hall, the floors seemed to be sloping up in front of her, making the distance almost impossible to traverse. She sat down for a second on the wooden steps of the hall and took a breather, listening out for Tink. She could hear voices, but the sound was impossible to locate in the cavernous hall. She got up again, almost toppling down the stairs, but somehow managing to ease herself down while clinging to the bannister. Once safely on the ground floor she began to search the rooms. The voices stayed with her, audible but not intelligible, before falling silent. Finally, she reached the rear of the house, bursting through heavy oak doors and blinking in the glare of the evening sunlight.

******

Her mother and Lacy hastily pulled apart, and as Tink advanced towards them, she felt tears welling up in her eyes.

'Where's Chris?' she demanded.

'He's gone love. We talked about this this morning,' said Tink.

'You let him drive? He was shitfaced.'

'Caz, don't swear.'

She couldn't believe it. Tink had dumped Chris and let him go off like that. She imagined him dead at the side of a road.

Lacy stood, hands hanging by his side, thumb furiously ticking off the milliseconds. Mumbling something about Rosie, he left the room, leaving Caz and Tink alone.

Caz gripped the watch in her pocket with hot sweaty fingers and bit hard so that she could feel the pressure in her teeth. She looked out of the window. Plump clouds had drifted down coming to rest on the horizon. Softly illuminated by the setting sun, they glowed smug and pink. Caz looked back at Tink, black spots blotching her vision.

'You do know Rosie is faking it, don't you?'

Tink pushed a piece of her hair behind her ear and shook her head.

'Caz, she didn't move at all for two days. Don't you think if she was faking it, she'd be running around by now?'

'But she is running around, she was just standing over me like some weirdo when I woke up, holding that freaky doll.'

'Love, Rosie's been down here with me for the past hour,' Tink said in the calming voice she used with people who'd lost their grip.

The room rolled backwards, and Caz squeezed the watch harder.

'That's not true. Since we got here, she's gone completely bonkers, she goes out into the woods and does some weird voodoo. She's not the same, she's being really really weird.'

'Love.' Tink put her arm around Caz and pulled her onto a sofa. 'Have you ever thought that you might be the one who's being weird? I mean, I know I haven't had much time for you and you've been angry about that. So don't you think you're having a bit of a strop?'

Caz bucked Tink's comforting arm from her shoulders and sat on the edge of the cushion. She picked up a paper knife from the table in front of her, testing the dull edge against her finger.

'You must think I'm a horrible mum. Letting you run wild and fend for yourself half the time,' Tink said in a wheedling voice that crept into Caz's chest and twisted itself in a knot around her heart.

'No mum, I think you're great,' she dutifully responded in a dull voice, her tears drying into a film that pinched her cheeks. She began etching patterns into the sofa with the knife.

'That's right, I think it's great that you can go out and have adventures without me. I do worry, but I'd hate to be one of those fussy mums who always wraps up their kids in cotton wool.'

'You do know, don't you?' said Caz, mimicking Tink's patronising tone.

'Know what?' Tink's voice was dreamy. She twirled a strand of Caz's hair in her fingers.

'About Sophie, the missing girl.'

Tink frowned and her soft dreamy demeanour hardened as her eyes focused properly on Caz. She pulled her hands back onto her lap.

'Of course, he told me about it. He's had a really hard time of it these past few years, losing his daughter and then his wife like that. I can't imagine what I'd do if I were in his place. If anything ever happened to Rosie...' she trailed off for a second. 'Or either of you two, I wouldn't know what to do with myself.'

'But what if something was about to happen to Rosie that morning she got lost? What if we arrived just in time? I mean he never called the police, did he? Wouldn't a normal person do that?' Caz said, stabbing the fabric to drive her point in.

'Love,' she said.

Her tone was soft and soothing, but she wasn't able to meet her daughter's eye, instead her gaze slid away over onto the table.

'Rupert and I have talked about this, he told me about all of it that night we had the party, you remember? You don't know how much he's suffered. You know right that I'm really attuned to people. I can sense when someone's not quite right and I'm 100 percent certain that he's sound. We can really trust him.'

'Why did he run off to Japan then?'

'Love, you have to learn that things aren't always what they seem. When you're older you'll understand. It was no accident that Rosie found her way here. This place has a lot of bad vibes, a lot of bad energy and we're here to help Rupert break out of that. You know I have very good instincts about these things.'

'I don't see why we can't we just call grandma and granddad and go home,' Caz said, pressing the knife down hard into the velvet.

'We've been over and over this. They're old. We can't always be putting stress on them.'

'You're just running away. You always do that when you don't like something. You did that with Chris. Grandma and granddad didn't want us to leave, we didn't want to leave. You think I liked living with a bunch of rats and head cases. Now you want us to live with a murderer.'

Caz kept the knife pressed deep into the fabric and twisted it round. Tink took hold of Caz's hand and took the knife away from her.

'You know what I think? I think you're working yourself up. I'm sorry I didn't notice. I thought you were okay, that that time when dad left was just a one off, but you know you're really getting over emotional again. You should really see yourself. It's hard being a single mum, I don't notice everything and I guess I don't want to smother you either, so I didn't see the signs.'

'I'm fine. You're the one who's going loony,' shouted Caz.

'Let me look at your hair,' Tink said, taking hold of Caz's head.

Caz pushed her away and stood up.

'Don't touch me. I hate you,' she shouted.

'Just calm down Caz. Tell me honestly, have you been pulling out your hair again?'

Caz picked up a plate that lay on the table and threw it against a wall, letting out a wild scream as she did so.

'I won't stay here. I hate you.'

Tink tried to restrain her, but Caz simply pushed her mother over back onto the sofa. She'd grown taller than Tink, and stronger.

'I hate you.'

She picked up another plate.

'Don't touch that, it isn't ours,' shouted Tink.

Before Caz got the chance to throw it, someone held her hand back. It was Lacy. She bit his arm. He didn't react but held her firmly. She squirmed and tried to escape but couldn't. He took the plate off her and placed it on the table, while still holding her still.

'Catherine, please calm down, you're upsetting your mother and Rosie. They're very worried about you. I know you didn't want Chris to leave.'

His breath smelt terrible to her, like something had crawled inside his mouth and died.

'Let me go.'

'You promise to calm down?'

'Let me go,' she repeated, letting go of the watch and pulling her hand out of the pocket so she could push away with both hands. It fell out onto the floor with a thud.

'What's this? Where did you get this?' Lacy asked.

'Where did you get it?' parroted Tink.

'It belonged to my mother.' Lacy's eyes were rimmed with red.

Caz looked at the watch on the floor. She felt a hot flush of shame, she had never ever stolen anything before and here she was, already caught.

'Caz, what did I teach you about stealing?'

'Property is theft,' she said, shoulders slumped, head hung in shame.

She started crying again, hot tears streaming down her face, the hard thing in her throat melted into a mush of self-pity and remorse.

CHAPTER EIGHTEEN

L ast time she'd got like this they'd had to shave her head. Nobody teased her at school because a rumour had gone round that she had cancer. She didn't bother to explain that she'd pulled great chunks of hair out herself. That she woke in the morning to a pillow covered in curly red hair. It wasn't until she started taking the medicine that her hair had grown back.

She sat up in bed and stared at the tiles surrounding the cold metal fireplace. A blue boy on a blue bridge was offering a bouquet of blue flowers to a blue girl. Below, a blue farmer was walking his blue dog while smoking a blue pipe. Pretty garlands of flowers, cats, milk maids all painted in cool blue on white ceramic. The little pill she had been given to calm her down and send her to sleep while it was still light outside had been blue too.

The weather had cooled down. Blown by a fresh breeze, fluffy white clouds slowly drifted through the sky, as mild as a flock of sheep. She picked up her book and began to read but couldn't remember where she'd got up to and when she flicked back a few pages, the story was like something half remembered from a dream. She put it down and stared back out at the clouds.

It had been grandma who had taken her to the doctor that other time. Caz wondered why Tink even had a supply of the pills grandma had given her then. It was so long ago, and she couldn't remember her mother being involved. She'd been too preoccupied with reading yellowing girl's annuals and listening to Janis Joplin loud in her bedroom. *Take another little piece of my heart now baby.*

There was a gentle knock and Tink entered the room, slipping sideways through the door and immediately shutting it behind her, like she was a spy infiltrating enemy territory. She crept towards the bed, ready to leap back to safety in case Caz had another hysterical fit. Easing herself into a chair, her eyes searched Caz's face for warning signs.

'How are you doing, love?' she asked, lightly stroking her daughter's face with her finger, afraid to stretch out her whole hand.

Caz didn't flinch like normal, her mother's touch felt gentle, soft, like a feather grazing her skin.

'Sleepy. I think,' said Caz. Her own voice sounded foggy, far away.

You look knackered love, you just stay in bed today and chill out for a bit, eh.' The soft tone didn't aggravate Caz anymore, she liked it. It was like being wrapped up in cotton wool.

'I brought you up a glass of water and a bit of a toast. Sit up for a sec and get it down you, then you can take another pill.'

She ate the bread. It felt like eating cardboard, but somehow, she got it down and swallowed another tiny pill, then lay back and looked at the ceiling. A fly was circling round and round the light shade. She stared at it. It would be nice to look at the blue people and the clouds again, but it was an effort to even lift her head. Finally, she closed her eyes and fell back asleep.

All day she fell in and out of a deep dreamless sleep. It was like she was stuck in a great lake of mud; she'd poke her nose above the surface now and then, like a hippo coming up for air, then sink back down into oblivion. At some point she ate a meal – white bread sandwiches with fish paste that stuck to the roof of your mouth and chocolate Angel Delight slurped off a huge spoon that was almost too heavy to hold – boo boo food that was as squelchy and gloopy as the texture of her sleep.

Bringing her knitting, Mrs Dixon stayed awhile and told Caz

something about Lady Diana, the Timotei shampoo advert and her sister's hip operation. The words seemed to float in the air and become muddled up, only a few making an impression in Caz's consciousness, so that there seemed to be no sense to what was said to her. It was nice, letting your grip on the world soften. Things didn't fall apart if you weren't constantly grasping at them, they just gently unravelled and disappeared into thin air.

The last time she surfaced that day, she found that the sky had deepened to an inky blue, the moon a tiny nick of silver, distant, pure. There was a knock on the door. She sat up in bed and switched on the lamp, squinting blearily in the light.

'Come in.' Her own voice sounded small.

It was Lacy, standing bowed in the doorway, thumbing the polished handle and frowning down at her.

'Ah.' A strange sound came from inside his throat as he struggled to dislodge the phlegm caught inside. 'Feeling a little better?'

Caz lifted her hands to her face and pressed the skin around her mouth with her fingertips as if to check. Her flesh felt like Plasticine.

'Yes. Thank you,' her voice said from somewhere far far away. It wasn't only her voice; she too was distant, diminished. But maybe she'd simply shrunk down to the right size.

Lacy walked inside and sat down in the chair next to Caz's bed then leaned in to inspect her.

'Perhaps we can be friends now, hmmm?' he said, leaning so close that she could smell that odd sweet, rotting scent on his breath.

She looked at her hands contritely folded on the duvet in front of her. 'I'm sorry for taking the watch. I was going to put it back. I just thought it was pretty,' Caz lied, scared that if she told him she'd needed it to run away with, he'd be mad at her again.

He stared at her for a moment and then took something out of his pocket and poured it onto the duvet. The chain made a shivering metallic noise. His thumb pulsed against the now empty fingers.

'A peace offering.' He coughed and laughed.

She nodded and reached out for it. He placed his large white hand over hers.

'You might want to keep this our little secret. Your sister might get jealous if she finds out.' His thumb began to turn, stroking her hand gently, his fingers cold. 'I'm going to London in a few days, perhaps there's something you'd like me to buy for you.'

166

CHAPTER NINETEEN

The three of them were walking across the lawn together, Rosie in the middle holding onto Tink and Lacy's hands. Every few paces they lifted her up and she threw her head back and swung from their arms, laughing, lost in the moment. Caz held her thumb up to one eye, so that the flesh became see-through, and continued to watch them. It was as if she'd blown up in size like a balloon, the substance of her body stretched, flesh dissolving.

Large grey clouds raced across the sky. Lightheaded, Caz felt as if she could be blown away out of the window and up into the stratosphere, leaving them far behind. They'd get smaller and smaller until their heads were barely pinpricks.

'They act like you're not even there, like you don't exist. Do you think they'd notice if you just disappeared?'

Ronnie slipped his fingers through hers. They stood side by side for a while looking down on the others playing out in the sunshine. The day dazzled, she wanted to turn away and crawl back under the covers, but Ronnie held her there.

'First chance they get I expect they'll send you off to a private school somewhere, so they don't have to deal with you.' He squeezed her fingers. 'Sorry about the other day. I had to leave. My mum turned up. She was banging on about me helping her out with the hoover. You heard my signal though, right?' He paused and she could feel him looking at her. Ronnie whispered, 'The way you disappeared like that, I thought they'd really got rid of you, for good.'

He dropped her hand and walked over to her breakfast tray.

'Aha,' said Ronnie. 'What's this?'

He held up the pill she'd left untouched by her mug of tea.

Caz turned her back on the happy family scene below.

'Oh, it's nothing, Diazepam I think. I'm taking it for my moods. I used to have a problem and mum thinks that it might be coming back, so just to be on the safe side...' she trailed off. 'There's nothing wrong or anything,' she said, failing to convince herself. If that were true, she would have taken the pill.

'Jesus,' he whistled. 'Do you know what Diazepam is?'

Caz didn't reply.

'They give this stuff to crazy housewives, it dopes them up. It's Valium. My mate nicks it off his mum.'

'It's fine, I just need it for a little while. I haven't been sleeping.'

Ronnie gently replaced the pill on the tray and frowned at the little blue dot.

'So, you did get something from the house?' he prompted.

Caz brought the watch out from the drawer beside her bed and placed it on the duvet. He picked it up and examined it, prizing open the golden shell casing and winding up the spring. He held it to his ear, listening to the quality of its tick, as if he were an expert on time pieces.

'Great, now Rosie's back up walking again, maybe we can get her out to the village tomorrow or the day after. I'll lend you the fare to Barchester and we can go to the pawn shop when we get there.'

Caz interrupted him, 'Actually, he gave me it. Lord Lacy, I mean, it's a gift. He's not so bad, a bit creepy, but I suppose I'll get used to him. We might as well stay the summer here. I think I was freaking out a bit yesterday. I mean it's nice not to sleep in the van. That stuff we took at the party, actually I think it made me go a bit crazy, you remember, I heard something in the south wing. I mean that's why I'm taking these pills. I was losing it. I couldn't sleep.'

'How do you know that they haven't drugged you to keep you quiet? How do you know this watch isn't a bribe?'

'Don't be silly. Look, I told you I had a problem before. I don't really want to talk about it.'

'You don't want to talk about it. That makes sense.' Ronnie looked at her and nodded his head as if something had become crystal clear.

After Ronnie left, she tried to forget what he'd said. She took a set of clean clothes from her drawers and went in to have a shower. If they lived here, she could have a bath every day. There might be other nice things too. Lacy had said he would buy her a new dress in London.

Pink from the shower, she got dressed in freshly laundered clothes and drifted downstairs in a haze of peach scent. Outside, the wind whipped her hair into her face and her clean skin felt tight against her skull. She took a grubby scrunchy from round her wrist and looped her hair through it into a ponytail.

Rosie stood at the top of the grass slope, face tipped to the sky, one arm raised, tightly holding onto taut thread. Nearby, Tink and Lacy made cooing appreciative sounds as the kite twirled and swooped in the air.

'What's going on?' she said, running up behind Rosie.

Her words had broken the spell that kept the kite in the air. It fell with a thud onto the lawn. Rosie wheeled round and scowled at her sister.

'I'll get it,' she shouted, running off in the direction of the kite to avoid a confrontation.

The kite was impressive: a fierce looking face with bulging eyes and bunched fingers painted onto its surface. Stretched over a light frame of honey-coloured wood, the texture of the paper was slightly rough.

Lacy came up behind her and ran a finger over its surface. 'Washi.' He made a guttural sound of satisfaction in his throat, like a cat purring. 'Japanese paper, handmade, the frame is bamboo. Mmmm magnificent, isn't it?' he said, taking it and holding it up to the sky, so that its colours showed up more brightly.

'Magnificent,' he repeated dreamily. 'I'll show you how to fly her.'

'Ready?' he shouted. Rosie waved back.

Lacy began to run down the hill away from the house, and suddenly let go of the thing. It soared up into the air. He lifted his head, temporarily losing his nervous tick and stoop as he watched it swoop upwards. They headed back in silence, Caz couldn't think of anything to say and clearly neither could he. He sat down besides Tink and put his arm around her. Caz sat a little way apart, slightly beneath them facing forwards towards the kite so that she wouldn't have to make eye contact.

'Ronnie not around today then?' Tink's bangles chinked together as she tried to light up a cigarette.

Caz shrugged. 'How should I know?'

'Didn't he come up to see you earlier? He seemed worried about you.'

'Just leave it mum,' Caz snapped.

'Did you have a fight or something? Lover's tiff?'

Suze must have said something. Tink tittered then went back to trying to light her fag, swearing as the wind blew out the flame. Caz got up and walked away from them, her limbs stiff, trying to walk naturally, as if she hadn't been humiliated.

'Can I have a go?'

Rosie looked at her and shrugged sullenly. Caz took the wooden reel from Rosie's hand.

'This is really cool,' said Caz, sounding awkward. How long had it been since she had had a natural conversation with Rosie? Had they ever had a natural conversation?

They both watched the kite, thinking their different thoughts. It danced erratically in her hands, unpolished movements out of sync with the complex ballet executed higher up in the heavens by a wheeling flock of birds.

'We don't want you around, Rupert is just being nice,' whispered Rosie, her voice barely audible against the wind.

Caz tugged the kite string and it suddenly veered off course, dropping in the sky, swooping round the figures in the fountain and crashing down onto the top of Perseus' spear.

'You ruined it,' Rosie said.

Caz walked towards the torn kite. By the time she'd reached the lip of the fountain, huge raindrops had begun to spot the surface of the stone bowl. Facing out, she put her palms flat on the edges and boosted herself up, balancing precariously on her bum for a second, before swinging her legs over into the empty pool. Some of the stone crumbled away in her fingers.

'Get out of there, for god's sake. You'll break your neck,' shouted Lacy, running towards her.

'Bill can get it down later with a ladder.'

'But it'll get ruined in the rain,' Caz replied, one hand on a stone foot, ready to clamber over the frozen bodies.

Lacy didn't reply but sighed and stooped further forward, a clenched fist against the stone rim.

Caz reluctantly returned, dropping back down onto the grass and slinking past him, down the slope and away towards the woods. A shrinking feeling ran down her back. She was a stick figure diminishing gradually, but not as quickly as they'd like, into the distance. Prickly as a cactus, she didn't fit into this soft lush landscape. She broke things, she clashed. The pills were to soften her up, they would stuff her out of sight, her sense of self slowly dissipating. Entering the wood, she snapped off a branch and began to whip the leaves about her, turning her anger outwards. She wouldn't bend this time, something else had to give.

Punching through the cardboard that had been taped up against the smashed pane of glass, she slid open the lock. The only way to get any purchase was to stick her hand inside the frame and pull up; a jagged piece of glass cut her palm as she was doing so. Leaving bloody smears on the ledge, she climbed in through the window. The room was the same as they had left it. Ronnie hadn't emptied the ashtray of roaches, so she guessed he didn't expect anyone in there.

The box of tapes had been left in the cupboard. It was an old tin. On its lid was a picture of a train made out of colourful biscuits. A rabbit dressed in a blue ticket inspector's cap was standing on the brightly-coloured biscuit-paved platform. Someone had gouged the rabbit's eyes out with a sharp object. She prized off the lid and worked her way through the box, found a copy of Gold Mother by James then popped it on the stereo.

As the music kicked in, she got comfortable on the sofa and checked out the rest of the box. A handful of tapes labelled with a spidery hand caught her attention: *Safari, Plane Crash, Medical Emergency, Moon Landing, Kidnapping*. Curious, she took out the album and slotted the first into the boom box. Someone's heavy breathing could be heard against the background hiss. A boy began talking.

'I'm here at Brackleigh Safari Park, with animal trainer Miss Portia Mew, the big cat expert.' A little girl giggled in the background. 'She's here to show us some of the most rabid lions and tigers in captivity. Hello Miss Mew.'

The voice was higher pitched, but there could be no doubt that the boy was Ronnie. The girl giggled and breathed, 'Hello,' into the microphone.

'Can you tell me something about these dangerous creatures Portia?'

'Well,' Sophie's breath thudded against the microphone, Ronnie was holding it close to amplify her voice. 'This here is a tiger and she's called, erm, Tiger and she'll eat you.'

'She'll eat me?' Ronnie laughed.

'Yes,' said Sophie seriously. A disgruntled cat meowed and Sophie screamed. 'Oh my God it's going for you.'

The other tapes were similar, an airplane suddenly out of control, about to crash, a conversation between mission control and a brave astronaut… It was strange listening to the dead girl like this. For some reason, Caz didn't feel scared. She was just another little girl, playing make believe with her friend. She and Rosie had had a short phase of doing the same thing. That was before Caz got bored of it. She was about to put the music back on when she noticed a different tape. Written in a neater hand, this one was titled *Twist*. Caz slipped it into the tape recorder.

Again, that heavy breath knocking against the mic, then

the girl began to sing: *Round and round the garden, like a teddy bear, a one step, a two step a tickly under there.* There was a faint click and the quality of the background hiss changed. 'No I won't go in there, I won't,' Sophie whispered. A sharp scream cut into this: 'No daddy, no!' Then an eerie giggle and the whole sequence looped round. She'd heard this before, that night in the south wing. Ronnie had made a compilation of Sophie's dialogue to scare her. The boom box had two tape decks, it would have been simple to rerecord parts of the other tapes.

As she sat listening, she heard the key in the door. She stood up and looked for someone to hide, then realised that she wasn't the one who'd just been caught in the act. The taped spooled round. 'Daddy, no!'

Caz stopped the recording and pressed eject, pocketing the tape. Ronnie didn't say anything, just stood in the doorway.

'That was a pretty sick trick to play on me.'

'You freaked out,' he confirmed, smiling at her. 'I wish you could have seen your face. In fact, I wish I had a camera now. It was classic.'

'You were trying to scare me away. You don't want us here,' said Caz. 'That's why you wanted to help me run away.'

Ronnie kicked the door with his foot, his hair falling forward, completely obscuring his face. His foot thumped rhythmically against the frame. Caz found herself thinking of those scratched out eyes on the biscuit tin. Would he do something to her if she pushed him too far? It would be dangerous to go against him, but if she kept him as an ally, they might both get what they wanted.

'If you want to get rid of us, you're going about it all wrong,' she found herself saying.

CHAPTER TWENTY

Lacy set off for London around two in the afternoon, promising to be back before ten that night. Once he had driven off, the others scattered like woodlice, burrowing away into different corners of the house. Tink went to the library where, wreathed in smoke, she read with her knees drawn up close to her body. Rosie retreated to the back of the house to lose herself in private fantasies spun out of whispered conversations with her dolly. Mrs Dixon went down to the kitchen and busied herself with more worldly tasks.

Caz and Ronnie stayed outside for a while, watching as Lacy's car disappeared down the driveway. The stone-grey sky drained the world of colour, making everything appear two dimensional and flat. Reflecting the blank cloud above, the windows of Upton Park looked unfocussed, as if, without Lacy, the building was drifting off into a deep slumber.

The gloomy weather seemed to signal a return to dull dependable normality, but was it possible that she could break the spell that had fallen over Rosie and Tink and return them all to their peaceful life in Radlett? Her memories of her previous life had faded in the intense glare of that weird summer and when Caz thought about school life, she could only conjure up flimsy dull images.

Once the sound of Lacy's engine died away, Caz stood up and clapped her hands, brushed the dirt from the seat of her trousers and headed off alone into the house in search of Rosie, leaving Ronnie behind on the step. Turning their plan over in her head, she slid on a loose slab in the dark hallway, falling backwards and spraining her wrist against the wall.

Just like the first morning they'd come to Upton Park, Rosie was nestled in a window ledge, whispering away conspiratorially to her Cindy doll. She stiffened and cut the secret conversation short when Caz entered.

'Hey,' said Caz, dragging her feet as she walked across the room and falling with a heavy sigh into a chair nearby. 'What're you up to?'

Rosie gripped the doll's plastic hands between thumb and fingertip. Caz sighed heavily again and stared up at the cracked plaster in the lofty ceiling.

'So, do you want to hear a secret?' Caz said, turning towards her sister.

Rosie remained silent, intent on running her fingers through the doll's nylon hair. The clock in the corner ticked off the empty seconds. Caz got out the watch Lacy had given her, opening and closing it with a loud snap, while at the same time kicking her toe against the table leg in front of her. Out of sync, the snapping and thumping were hard to ignore, but Rosie kept staring at her doll, straining to pretend that her sister wasn't there.

'No, oh well...' Caz stopped kicking the chair and pocketed the watch, then pushed herself up and began to walk lazily towards the door.

'You don't know any secrets,' whispered Rosie.

'Oh really? I know more than you think. While you've been sick in bed, I've been wandering all over. This house is full of secrets. I know about Lacy's sword collection, that's why he gave me this.' Caz brought out her shell watch and shoved it under Rosie's nose. 'To shut me up. He doesn't want mum knowing about it. But that's not the secret I was going to tell you.'

Rosie glared at her, obviously annoyed that Caz had received a gift from Lacy.

'You stole that. You never got anything from him,' she said.

'Didn't I? Why don't you ask him when he gets back? He'll tell you. He was just worried you'd get jealous.' Caz looked into the mirror over the fireplace and pouted, plumping her curls coquettishly with her palm.

Rosie had begun pressing the sides of her doll's head so that its features ballooned outwards.

'But this other secret, you've got to promise, cross your heart hope to die, that you won't tell Lacy. It's about the little girl, Sophie, the girl you were looking for in the woods.'

'Sophie?' Rosie said, turning to her sister.

'That's her name, didn't they tell you?'

'Mrs Dixon said that there was a little girl, a girl that got lost and that's why Mr Lacy got sad. She told me never to talk to him about it. I thought if I could find her...'

'But she isn't lost, that's the thing. She's in this house,' Caz said whispering as if someone might be listening in.

She drew closer to Rosie, leaning near the window ledge, her ginger curls spiralling down over her sister's head. 'There's a way you can see her, but you've got to do what I say, and you can never ever tell mum or Mr Lacy about it.'

******

As they crept towards the door that led to the south wing, Rosie hung close to her sister, gripping the back of her t-shirt in her fist, the same way she'd done when they'd first entered the round house. Caz remembered when her sister had been born. Remembered her tiny bunched up fingers, how helpless she'd looked.

The slight chill that pervaded the old stone house seemed to intensify in the south wing, perhaps because the curtains were permanently drawn against the light outside. The corridor was dark except for a sickly-looking rhomboid of daylight that spilled out from the door at the end.

As she passed the door to the room with the four-poster bed, Caz pushed aside the memory of what had happened there.

It squirmed nastily at the edges of her consciousness, refusing to fit into any neat logical picture. Surely it couldn't have been Sophie standing over her like that? It had to have been Rosie, but she couldn't ruin the plan by confronting her.

'We're not allowed in here,' said Rosie.

'That's exactly why you're not allowed to tell anyone that we've been here. I mean it, mum and Lacy will be furious with you,' replied Caz, pushing open the door.

The room had no curtains and was bare of furniture except for a large chest of drawers that stood against one wall. A bin liner had been left on the floor, its contents half regurgitated. Socks, pinafore dresses, blouses: Sophie's things. On the floor, Caz had laid down an Indian scarf and set up a little altar, similar to the one that Rosie had made in the woods, on top. She knelt down on the floor and lit a candle, waving it theatrically around in the air. Rosie knelt beside her. Caz took this as her cue to pick up the cup she'd prepared and hand it to Rosie.

'You have to drink this to find her.'

'Why, what is it?' said Rosie, looking doubtful.

'You remember the night of the party? Well, I took some of that red drink they were all having. Me and Ronnie came here and that's how I found her.' Caz held out a cup filled with black-currant squash.

'It tastes bad,' said Rosie, taking a little sip.

'That's because it's strong medicine, it helps you to cross over into her world.'

She put her hands together.

'Now for the incantation: 'Sophie Sophie come out to play,' she whispered. 'You say the same.'

They chanted together, calling out to Sophie. Caz opened one eye and looked at her sister, wondering if Rosie felt as terrified as she did.

'Okay, that should be enough to get her attention. Now you have to go through the portal,' Caz said, opening up the small square-shaped hatch in the wall that Ronnie had showed her. She had brought some cushions along, so the bottom of the closet was well padded. Rosie would have to draw her feet up, but it was large enough for her to sit up straight inside, her soft blonde hair grazing the top.

'You have to promise that you won't tell a soul about this. Sophie told me that no adults can know. It's not possible for adults to enter through the portal to her reality. Rupert wouldn't understand, he'd think you were lying,' Caz said. 'There's only room for one. But don't be afraid, I've been through here before. What you have to do now is keep your eyes shut tight and just keep calling out Sophie's name in your head. She'll find you.'

Rosie climbed in, settling herself amongst the cushions Caz had placed there earlier. Caz stroked her hair. 'It's really a wonderful place. I know you'll like it there. Don't you remember when we read The Lion, the Witch and the Wardrobe? It's like that. You can stay as long as you like because time works differently. It might even be winter in there, so here.' She picked up a sweater from the clothes strewn on the floor. 'This will keep you warm. Just close your eyes and call out to her,' assured Caz. 'I'll be here waiting for you.'

'I'm sorry I was mean to you Caz,' said Rosie, lying back and closing her eyes.

She looked so sweet, so adorable. Caz shut the door gently and sat and waited, watching treetops churn in the wind outside. She looked at her watch. It was three thirty.

Outside, the sky was full of dark clouds. A swell of seaweed-tinted grey that threatened to spill over and flood the grounds below. In anticipation of a downpour, the sea monster writhed in the fountain and grimaced conspiratorially up at Caz. She leaned back against the wall and stared at the door. Raindrops gently tapped on the window outside. She turned away and found herself looking at the black plastic bag. It looked lumpen, horrid, as if something nasty was about to crawl out. The image of Sophie standing over her wormed its way back into her mind. She'd given Rosie too many blue pills, Sophie's angry jealous ghost would snatch away Rosie's life, she would stand over her so she couldn't move and suffocate her with that horrible doll...

After 30 minutes had passed, she opened the door. Rosie's head was lolling sideways, her mouth open as she dreamed.

'Rosie,' she whispered and then again, loudly, 'Rosie.'

No response. She poked her sister and still Rosie didn't react. The little blue pills had done their job. She picked up the walkie-talkie and switched it on, the noise of crackling static made her start, and she could hear her heart beating wildly in her ears. She pushed the red button.

'Stage one complete, I repeat, stage one complete.'

The coded messages they'd thought of struck her now as being a little childish.

She gathered the bits and bobs she'd put out on the altar into a plastic bag and sat and waited. After about ten minutes she heard the door opening down the hall followed by footsteps. Her heart pounded and she had the ridiculous idea that Sophie's ghost would enter the room. The doorknob turned. It was Ronnie, of course.

'She's fast asleep,' whispered Caz.

'Do you think we gave her enough? Maybe we ought to tie her up? Just to make sure she doesn't make any noise when they come looking for her,' Ronnie whispered back.

Caz frowned. 'We're not tying her up.'

She shut the door, hearing a tiny click as the metal catch fell into place, then stood up and took one end of the heavy desk of drawers.

'You sure about this? If they discover her like this, the shit will really hit the fan,' said Ronnie.

'But I'll be the one to blame, right? Rosie will never know you were a part of it. Let's just get it over with and move this thing,' she hissed.

After they'd moved it in front to hide the door, they sneaked out of the room and went back into the main building.

Back in her room Caz picked up her book, but the noise of the house creaking as the wind moaned outside her window unsettled her. Her window rattled as if something was trying hard to get in. The swollen clouds overhead darkened, ready to burst and drench the grounds below. With her Walkman on, she could drown out the terrible noise of the wind wailing outside, but it was impossible to forget about Rosie trapped in that tiny closet, banging on the walls in a panic, desperate to get out, or, worse, dying of an overdose.

Despite these thoughts, a conviction that this was the only way to leave the house kept her from dashing out of the room, down the corridors and pulling Rosie out. She began tidying away her few possessions: folding clothes, matching socks, stacking books and picking up junk from the carpet – getting ready to leave.

When she'd finished, she went and retrieved a deck of cards from Rosie's room and began playing solitaire. It had got so dark outside that it felt as if it were much later. Caz had taken off her digital watch and placed it face down in front of her, so she wouldn't keep checking the time, but it didn't do much good, her hand kept automatically searching for the thing, flipping it over to show that only a minute or so had passed since the last time she'd checked. Time crawled so slowly that it barely seemed to move at all and every time she checked the watch, she discovered that what had felt like five minutes had actually been only one. Her personal sense of time was grossly out of kilter with reality. The odd jolt she experienced each time she checked her watch was like the lurching sensation you get when you realize the train you're in isn't moving at all, it's just the train next to you pulling out of the station. Sickened, she finally threw the watch on top of the wardrobe.

It seemed like an eternity before the timid knock came at Caz's door.

'Caz, it's time for dinner,' Tink gently intoned. 'Caz?'

Caz pretended to be lost in her game of solitaire. 'Uh huh,' she replied.

Tink entered the room.

'Have you seen Rosie? She's not in her room.'

'No. I haven't seen her since Lacy left for London, just after lunch.'

Tink looked around the room and flapped her arms up and down uselessly, like a penguin that didn't realise it couldn't fly.

'Perhaps she's with Mrs Dixon? Maybe they're in the kitchen?' Caz remarked, snapping a card down.

'No, no, Mrs Dixon just called me for dinner. She said she hadn't seen Rosie either.'

'Curiouser and curiouser. I hope she isn't playing hide and seek, we'll never find her in this house,' said Caz, looking up and raising an eyebrow.

'She was with me for a moment after we said goodbye to Rupert and then she just sloped off. You know how she is.'

'Insane,' said Caz, putting down another card.

******

Walking up and down the corridors of the main building, they sang out Rosie's name, the way you do to a timid pet at feeding time. The only response was the wind screaming back an empty reply.

'Wo-sie- it's dinner time, we've got your favourite food,' Tink cooed down long lonely corridors and into empty rooms.

'Maybe she's mad that she didn't get to go to London. If we carry on looking for her, we might be here for hours. Remember the time she hid under the bathroom sink? We should just eat, she'll come out when she's hungry.'

Tink nodded, relieved that Caz was also willing to give up the search. Rosie had a legendary stubborn streak, but she always surfaced eventually.

The rain started up as they began to tuck into their beans on toast. Caz was relieved that with Lacy out of the picture, they wouldn't be forced to eat anything more elaborate. The beans were going cold, but Caz had a huge appetite and wolfed down her meal. Tink only ate half and ended up gazing out at the streaks of rain running down the windowpane, twisting her hair in her fingers.

'I hope Rosie's not out in this, she'll catch her death,' she said.

'I'm SURE she's inside mum,' reassured Caz.

'I'm a terrible mother letting you all run free like this. But you know I always felt like I had a straitjacket on when I was a little girl. I could never get my dresses dirty, mum used to make me wear the most ridiculous outfits, no good for playing outside. Everything was about what other people thought of us, I always thought it'd be better to live without caring what anyone thought of you, to just enjoy yourself and you know, sod the next-door neighbours.'

'Mmm huh,' nodded Caz.

'You don't know how lucky you are not having a fussy mother looking over your shoulder all the time, being able to run around where you like, getting your clothes dirty. I've always thought you're so sensible and that's probably because you've always been independent. I'm very proud of you you know,' Tink continued.

The clocked ticked. A formless whirl of rain and wind sounds rushing in the spaces between, making the interval between seconds seem to expand and contract.

'Perhaps we should look for her again,' said Tink, half getting to her feet.

'She'll just want to keep hiding if we're looking for her, let's just wait a bit more,' Caz said, turning on a lamp.

Tink sat back down again. The portraits on the wall turned their noses up and their mouths down in permanent disapproval.

'This house is so lonely, it kind of swallows you up. I wonder how Mr Lacy stood it here all by himself. It just goes to show you doesn't it, that having lots of things doesn't bring happiness. Rupert feels like he's responsible for all this stuff, but what does it give him in return? It drags him down that's what. The poor man has been sinking. He can't afford to keep this place up, that's why I've been trying to convince him to sell it to the National Trust or something,' said Tink.

A loud crash in the hallway made them jump out of their

skins. They ran out to see what the matter was. It was Mrs Dixon, who'd dropped the empty tray she'd been carrying on the stone floor. Caz's blood thudded as it pulsed through her ears. Feeling dizzy, she sat down on the step.

'I'm all fingers and thumbs,' said Mrs Dixon, her beetroot red face turning purple as she bent to pick up the tray.

'We thought you might be Rosie,' said Tink.

'She still not turned up? Oh my goodness.' Mrs Dixon wiped away the wet strands of wispy hair off her forehead with the back of her meaty hand.

'Caz thinks she's hiding.'

'It's just a theory,' said Caz.

'We've got to search the house then. If she's gone into the south wing and turned on a switch, she might have electrocuted herself, or fallen through some rotten floorboards. Sorry, I don't want to worry you, but it isn't safe in there.' Mrs Dixon's eyes were rolling around in her head as she said this, like a fish caught in a net.

'Me and Ronnie can look for her in there,' said Caz.

'You'll do no such thing. I'll get Bill to go in, he's still about and he knows that part of the house better than anyone. You two can go off to the woods to check the round house. I'll give you both some rain gear, so you won't get drenched.'

******

Looking like spacemen in raincoats, rubber trousers and oversized wellington boots, Ronnie and Caz set off across the lawn. Caz gripped the large waterproof torch in her left hand, on the side closest to Ronnie. When he moved closer, she swung her arm back and forth, sending the beam juddering up and down the lawn. Ronnie fell behind and caught back up with her, moving to her right-hand side, she switched the torch over into her other hand so he wouldn't be able to grasp hold of her fingers. It was stupid, but she felt mad with him about Rosie's disappearance, as if the whole thing had been his idea. Luckily with the rain lashing their faces and the wind howling in their ears, it wasn't possible for them to discuss any of it until they got inside the round house and thunked the door shut behind them.

They were quiet for a while, removing their raincoats and sitting down opposite one another in the lounge, adjusting to the depth of silence inside the still house.

'Don't worry,' Ronnie reassured her. 'Bill doesn't know about the cupboard in the wall. It's something I found myself with Sophie ages ago. I don't even think Rupert knows about it.'

Caz looked away from Ronnie and picked up a blue plastic carrier bag that had been left by the side of her chair.

Inside was the rag doll.

'Where did this come from?' she asked.

'I pulled it down from the shelf the other day.'

It grinned at her and Caz dropped it to the floor. She had been sure that it had been Rosie, standing over her with the doll in her hands, but the doll had stayed stuffed in a bag the whole time. If that was true, then her mum had been probably been right, Rosie had been downstairs the whole time. The whole thing had been a dream or... A cold panic passed over her. The round house felt like it was turning.

'We should turn the lights on upstairs, to show we're looking.' She jumped up and raced up the stairs towards the top bedroom.

The south wing stood dark as usual above the trees. Caz gripped the windowsill, scared that Bill had found Rosie and scared that he hadn't.

'We should have given her more pills like I said,' said Ronnie, coming up behind her. He slipped his arm around her waist. Caz felt like she couldn't breathe. 'She might be banging on the wall right now, trying to get out,' he added.

Caz looked out of the window, felt the cold glass close to her skin.

'Have you always had keys to this house?'

'Of course, but I haven't really needed to go here much.'

'No?'

'No.'

'Where were you taking that rag doll, the other day when I bumped into you?'

'I thought Rosie might like it as a present. It used to belong to Sophie you know.'

Ronnie tried to pull her closer, but she pushed him away and ran off back to the house, grabbing just her raincoat and forgetting to take the torch. She fell over on the path through the woods, gashing her knee against a stone, the blood showing up black as she emerged out onto the lawn and limped back up to the house.

She arrived back in the hallway, shivering slightly. Tink and Mrs Dixon ran out to meet her.

'I, we couldn't find her,' said Caz, eyes filling up with tears.

Mrs Dixon walked up to her and gave her a hug, squashing her against her upholstered form. Caz let the tears run more freely and hugged Mrs Dixon back.

'Let's get that knee seen to,' she said, trying to steer Caz in the direction of her subterranean kitchen.

'No, I want to wait for Bill to come back down,' said Caz, sitting down in a hard wooden chair and putting her arms round herself. Tink came up to her and lightly stroked her shoulder.

'I suppose I can go and fetch my first aid kit from downstairs,' Mrs Dixon said, bustling off down the stairs.

'You didn't find anything?' asked Tink.

'No,' said Caz, angrily. 'I would have said, wouldn't I?'

Tink sighed and leaned against the wall. They both waited in silence for Bill to come back down the stairs. It was 8:15 according to clock in the hall.

Caz thought back to another time when Rosie had gone missing. She must have only been about five years old. They'd been in a theme park with grandma and granddad and suddenly Rosie disappeared. They searched all around, Caz crying her eyes out a little self-indulgently at the idea that her sister might be missing forever, imagining what all the other children at school would say. Eleanor would have to be nicer to her, now she'd lost her sister.

In the end, when they found Rosie happily eating a lolly-pop, being taken care of by the staff, completely oblivious to the stress she'd put them through, Caz had been so angry that she didn't speak to her for all the rest of the day. What made her really sick was the way her grandparents had fawned over Rosie, even though she'd been the one to run off and get lost. This time Rosie would stay lost until Caz wanted her to be found.

It was nearly nine when Bill came back down the stairs shaking his head. A feeling of relief that left a nasty aftertaste passed through Caz.

He took his cap off, then fixed his watery eyes on Tink.

'Aint there,' he said, barely moving his mouth.

Tink nodded and sighed.

'Don't look good, do it?'

Trying to dispel the gloom created by Bill's dark mutter-ings, Tink rushed to the phone. Lacy had left the number of his lawyer in London on a pad beside the telephone. She picked up the receiver, dialled the number and listened, frowning.

'I must have done it wrong,' she said, replacing the receiver and dialling again, but losing her grip on the dial halfway through. She slammed the phone down and tried again.

'It says 'number not recognised,' she said, frowning.

'Gives it here,' said Mrs Dixon, taking over the phone and firmly dialling through the numbers on the pad. She listened, a puzzled look on her face. 'Well, that is odd,' she said. 'I'm getting the same thing.'

No matter how many times they dialled they wouldn't be able to get through. Using the same pen, it had been easy for Caz to alter a six and a five into eights.

Nobody wanted to be the first to suggest calling the police. Finally, Tink squeaked, 'Do you know the name of his lawyer? Maybe we could call directory enquiries?'

Mrs Dixon turned to her. 'I don't, no. But don't you worry. Mr Lacy'll be back from London soon enough if the traffic isn't bad. Then all this will be cleared up.'

'We should wait though, right, before calling the police or anything, right?' Tink turned to look at Caz, her voice unsteady.

******

Caz had meant to be poised, ready for the moment when Lacy finally walked in the door, but she ended up lying sideways on the sofa and closing her eyes. She was staring at the square hatch in the wall. Something trapped behind was banging hard on the inside, so that the door shook every few seconds, louder and louder with more and more force until it burst open, a wave of butterflies shooting out past her, so that she staggered back, holding up her hands to her face.

Turning round, she found herself face to face with a pretty blonde girl in a silk Chinese dress. The butterflies that clung to her dress and hair trembled every so often. Caz peered closer and touched the teardrop-shaped wing of black and white butterfly, as she did so, it turned ash grey, its dry corpse crumbling in her fingers to a pile of dust. The girl too had turned to stone and was now disintegrating, trickling down onto the floor into a pile of sand. Caz looked back inside the hatch and found a small brown glass bottle. Bending down to read the label, the elegant letters swirled before her eyes in a playful dance. 'Chlo,' she read. 'Chloro...' The letters twirled away from her, the sound of their laughter tinkling against a crystal chandelier. 'Chloroform!' the dancers shouted.

She found herself in a huge glittering ballroom, filled with couples dancing. Suze swished past riding a bright pink flamingo. Waving a teapot in the air, she smiled at Caz and danced away. Trying to find an exit, Caz fought through the dancers, but the checkerboard floor seemed to stretch as far away as the eye could see and suddenly, she too was dancing with a partner; a very tall partner, wearing a white Japanese mask. It was Lacy. She tried to get away but couldn't, the mask grinned at her nastily and as she struggled, she realised that the man in the mask wasn't as tall as she had thought and not so strong either, sleek chestnut hair had fallen over his face, obscuring the mask, he flicked it out of his eyes and she woke, heart beating so fast it was hard to catch her breath.

She wiped saliva from her mouth and sat up. She could hear shouting outside in the hallway. She got up and stood, listening at the door.

'If you had an ounce of responsibility, you would have known where she was at all times. Almost unbelievable that you could lose track of her again. Wasn't it just last week that she turned up here, gone half the night, I suppose it's a blessing you realised she was gone at all before morning.'

'And look what happened that time, she turns up here, with you. I've always wondered why you didn't call the police that night you found her, that would have been the normal thing to do wouldn't it?'

Like most of the rooms in Upton Park, the lounge had more than one door, and this allowed Caz to leave the room undetected. She had to get Rosie out of there. A black cloud pressed at the edges of her vision as she ran as quietly as possible up the side staircase and crossed the landing above Tink and Lacy. Luckily, they were so busy arguing that they didn't notice her. Her luck held and she managed to slip unseen along the empty corridors and into the south wing, the cold doorknob rattling for a second in her trembling fingers.

The passage was darker now and she had to feel her way blind along the wall, stifling a scream when she finally bumped into the end of the corridor. Her fingers crawled along the wall and through the door to the switch. She flipped it and the room exploded into light, exposing Sophie's inanimate garments abandoned on the floor.

The dark mahogany chest of drawers sat with its back against the wall, solemnly guarding the entrance to the closet. Outside the wind howled; a giant injured beast trying to break down the house's stone walls, rattling and nearly shattering its fragile windows.

Caz grasped the top edge of the chest at one side with her

chilled fingers and strained her weight against it. It refused to budge, so she pushed harder, the chest protesting as its heavy legs dug into the floor. Each time she could only manage to move it a couple of inches, so that when she'd finally exposed the closet door, she was covered in sweat.

She wiped her palm over her wet forehead, leaned against the wall and placed her hand on the handle. It opened with a muffled click and the door swung wide.

Rosie wasn't there. The sight of the hollow cavity opened up a corresponding yawning space in her own chest. She paused, teetering on the brink of this abyss for a few seconds, then threw herself out of the room and hurtled down the corridor into the main house.

She had intended to crash land downstairs and spill her guts to Tink, but instead found herself following a twisted route along the corridors on the first floor, innards churning. She walked with her head down, staring at her feet, so she could avoid the accusing gaze of the rows of silent witnesses hung on the walls. Not looking where she was going, she nearly bumped into Ronnie, creeping out of the insect room with an empty plastic bag crushed in his hand. She recoiled and he smiled back at her brightly.

'Wow, chill out,' he said.

She stared at him, stupefied. A funny smell sweetened the air around him; his manner, too, was artificially saccharine.

'How about we go and get Rosie out now they're distracted?'

'She's gone,' Caz said.

As she spoke the words, she felt as if a gust of air had just flown through the hole punched inside her. She put her fingers up to her chest.

'Come off it,' Ronnie said, looking genuinely surprised.

'I just went in there to get her, and she's gone.'

Her throat hardened as she held back her tears.

'I thought we were going to get her out together. Why didn't you wait for me?'

Ronnie frowned and then looked up at her through his fringe.

'Is this some kind of trick you two cooked up to pay me back for the tapes?'

Caz stared at him and as she did so, the hole inside her seemed to bulge. The more she talked to him, the less certain she was of the truth. She almost found herself believing him. She had to act, not argue.

'I'm going to tell them what we did,' Caz said, before walking away.

'I'd like to see you try explaining why you drugged your sister and locked her in a closet,' he shouted after her.

******

With all the lights blazing, the hallway looked abandoned, reminding Caz of a grubby cinema suddenly illuminated after a film. The dusty mirrors, loose stone slabs and abandoned junk made her want to rush to the nearest exit so she could leave the whole mess behind her.

'She's been gone for seven hours. We've searched the whole house and now it's 10.30, it's dark outside, we just don't know what to do... Eight years old. Blonde hair, blue eyes... She was wearing, um.'

Tink had her back to Caz, fingers wound round the cream plastic spiral of the telephone cord.

'A blue dress with a flowery pattern,' prompted Caz, from behind.

Her mother repeated the description to the police. 'How long will you be? It's just I have another young daughter and we're here alone with him. Yes, I understand. Thank you.'

Even after the call had ended, Tink continued to grip the receiver in her fingers. Caz approached her mother carefully and took hold of her other hand.

'Shall we call grandma and granddad?' she suggested.

Finally giving in, Tink began to dial.

******

They waited in the front lounge for the police to arrive. Caz trying to think of a way to tell her mother what had happened, but no matter which way she spun the story, the finger of blame revolved back to point at her and the longer she maintained her silence, the more difficult it became to say anything. She looked down at her clenched fists and noticed coils of red hair snaking out between her fingers.

'I can't believe I didn't listen to you,' said Tink.

Shrivelled up with worry, she looked tiny in the large leather chair she was sitting in.

'I just didn't see it. I still can't believe it. I'm usually really good at reading people's vibes. God, I can't just sit here doing nothing. I should be out searching for her.'

Tink made as if to get up, but Mrs Dixon placed a plump hand on her frail shoulder and pushed her back into the seat.

'Mr Lacy is searching the house with Ronnie right now. You just sit yourself down there and try to stop fretting. You'll need to be here when the police turn up. Why don't I make some tea to calm our nerves while we wait?' said Mrs Dixon.

She left the room and they sat silent for a while, listening to the noise of the storm outside.

'I'm scared, Caz. The police will be on our side, won't they? I mean this is the second time, the second time that...' Tink said after a few minutes had passed. She obviously had trouble finding the words to describe what had happened.

'Honestly mum, I don't think anything. Rosie probably went off on a walk and got lost or something,' she said without conviction.

She stared out of the window, hoping to see a tiny rain drenched figure out on the lawn.

'If someone did take her, it's not necessarily Mr Lacy. I mean Ronnie was here too,' Caz said.

Her mother lifted her head and looked at her.

'Ronnie's been helping out his mother with the chores all afternoon, she told me so.' She turned her head and fixed Caz with a questioning look. 'Do you know something Caz?'

Mrs Dixon stood at the door holding a tray in her large beefy hands, looking at them both with the wild eyes of a dying fish, thin blonde baby hair twisting upwards as if lashed by a strong gale.

'I think the police are here,' she announced.

As they entered the hallway, Caz heard another noise above the wailing of the wind. The strange cry made her think of the time she'd come into the kitchen in the squat and found a rat dragging itself around the dirty vinyl floor, the lower half of its body flattened and gouged in one of the traps that had been left out. It had looked right at her, pink mouth open, emitting a horrible squealing noise. As if he, too, had been skewered in the guts, Lacy sat bent forward on the stairs, both hands holding his stomach. Ronnie sat beside him looking mildly bewildered, patting Lacy's shoulder. The action ridiculously inadequate for the situation.

Tink opened the door to the police and a cold blast of air blew through the house. The dark figures of the policemen standing in the doorway looked impossibly huge to Caz. She looked beyond them at the patrol cars parked in the driveway. Blue lights swung round the rain drenched garden intermittently illuminating the figures in the fountain. The sea monster's teeth glistened in the deluge and from that angle he appeared to be smiling, as if he had just devoured some tasty morsel.

ABOUT THE AUTHOR

Felicity Hughes is a writer and editor. As a journalist, she's delved into the seedier side of Japan for publications including The Guardian and The Japan Times. Now based in sunny Spain, she still writes about darker forces that lurk behind the scenes.

Did you enjoy this book?
Want to hear more from Felicity Hughes?
Check out her website at: www.felicityhughes.com

Printed in Great Britain
by Amazon